PURE MAGIC

Laura Shenton

PURE MAGIC

Laura Shenton

Iridescent Toad Publishing

Iridescent Toad Publishing.

Cover by ZoneArtz Design.

First edition. ISBN 978-1-917969-08-6

Chapter One
Welcome to Hell, Population: Me

The acceptance letter burst into purple flames the moment I finished reading it, which should have been my first clue that Ravenwood Academy for Advanced Witchcraft was going to be a pain in my arse.

"Congratulations, Ms Blackthorne," I muttered, sweeping the ash residue off my kitchen counter with the back of my hand. The smell of burnt paper and magic lingered in the air, mixing with the scent of the instant coffee I'd been nursing for the past hour. "You've been accepted to the most prestigious witch academy in the country. Please report for orientation on the first of September. Formal attire required."

Formal attire. Right. Because nothing says "I'm ready to learn magic" like wearing uncomfortable shoes and a dress that shows every sweat stain. I'd spent the last decade of my life actively avoiding anything that could be described as formal. My wardrobe consisted of ripped jeans, band t-shirts from concerts I'd snuck into, and a leather jacket I'd stolen from an ex who definitely deserved it.

Three months later, here I stood at the gates of Ravenwood, tugging at the hem of my plaid skirt – the only "formal" thing I owned that didn't make me look like I was attending a funeral or auditioning for a secretary position in 1952. The September wind whipped my black hair across my face, and I could already feel my carefully applied eyeliner starting to smudge. Twenty minutes of effort with makeup I rarely wore, wasted.

The academy loomed before me like something out of a gothic nightmare: all dark stone towers and narrow windows that watched you like eyes. Gargoyles perched on every corner, their stone faces twisted into expressions of perpetual judgment. The iron gates were at least twenty feet tall, decorated with intricate metalwork that formed shapes I didn't want to look at too closely – they seemed to move when you weren't watching directly.

"You lost, new girl?"

I turned to find three women standing behind me, each one looking like they'd stepped out of a fashion magazine for witches – if such a thing existed. The speaker, a blonde with perfectly coiffed hair and nails that could double as weapons, looked me up and down with the kind of disdain usually reserved for something you'd scrape off your shoe. Her lips were painted a perfect red.

"Nope," I said, shouldering my worn duffel bag that contained everything I owned in the world. "Just taking in the view before I head inside and dazzle everyone with my raw magical talent."

The blonde's companions – a redhead with a pixie cut that somehow made her look both elfin and dangerous, and a brunette who looked like she bench-pressed other students for fun – snickered. The brunette's arms were crossed, biceps visible even through her designer blazer.

"Raw magical talent?" The blonde stepped closer, and I caught a whiff of expensive perfume mixed with something else. Power.

It rolled off her in waves, making the air between us crackle with static electricity. "Let me guess. You're one of those charity cases they let in every year. What was it? Accidentally levitated your cat? Made flowers bloom out of season? Set fire to your diary when your crush didn't text you back?"

"Actually," I said, meeting her gaze without flinching, letting a small smile play at the corners of my mouth, "I set my ex-boyfriend's car on fire. With my mind. While he was in it. With his new girlfriend. Who happened to be my sister."

The snickering stopped abruptly, like someone had hit a switch.

"He survived," I added with a casual shrug that I'd practiced in the mirror. "Mostly. The eyebrows never quite grew back the same though. And my sister has this interesting scar pattern on her shoulder that looks like a phoenix. Very artistic, if I do say so myself."

The blonde's perfect mouth twisted into something that might have been a smile if smiles could kill. Her eyes – an icy blue that probably matched her heart – narrowed slightly. "I'm Victoria Ashford. These are my friends, Scarlett and Morgana. We run things here at Ravenwood."

"Fascinating," I said, stepping around them with deliberate casualness. "I'll be sure to remember that when I'm running things next week."

I made it three steps before Victoria's voice stopped me, sharp as a blade. "I don't think you understand how things work here, new girl. There's a hierarchy. A structure that's been in place since forever. And trust me, you're at the bottom of it. So far at the bottom you'd need a telescope to see the middle."

I turned back slowly, letting my own power – raw and untrained as it was – flare just enough to make the air around me shimmer with heat waves. The temperature rose ten degrees in a second. "Here's the thing, Victoria. I didn't come here to play mean girls with a bunch of privileged witches who think they're special because daddy bought them a spot at the top of the food chain. I came here to learn magic. Real magic. The kind that makes people nervous. So you can take your hierarchy and shove it somewhere uncomfortable."

"You little..."

"Ladies." A smooth male voice cut through the tension. "Is there a problem here?"

We all turned to see a man approaching from the main building. Tall, dark-haired, with the kind of jawline that could cut glass, and eyes the colour of storm clouds just before lightning strikes. He wore a charcoal suit that probably cost more than my entire wardrobe plus a year's rent, and he moved with the easy confidence of someone who knew exactly how devastating he looked. The kind of man who'd never had an awkward phase in his life.

"Professor Darkwood," Victoria said, her entire demeanour shifting from predator to teacher's pet in an instant. Her voice went from razor blades to honey. "We were just welcoming the new student. Making sure she felt... included."

His gaze shifted to me, and I felt something in my chest do a stupid little flip that I immediately decided to ignore. Up close, I could see flecks of silver in those storm-grey eyes, and a faint scar through his left eyebrow that somehow made him more attractive, not less.

"And you are?"

"Raven Blackthorne," I said, proud that my voice came out steady and not like I'd swallowed a handful of butterflies. "New girl. Pyrokinetic with a bad attitude, according to my acceptance letter. Also, apparently I have 'untapped potential that could either save or destroy everything I touch'. They really went all out with the character assessment."

His lips twitched in what might have been amusement. "They put that in writing?"

"I may be paraphrasing. Slightly. The actual letter might have used terms like 'concerning volatility' and 'requires immediate intervention'."

"Well, Ms Blackthorne, welcome to Ravenwood. I'm Professor Damien Darkwood. I teach Advanced Defensive Magic." He glanced at Victoria and her crew with a look that suggested he saw right through their innocent act. "I trust Ms Ashford and her friends were being... hospitable?"

"Oh, absolutely," I said, giving Victoria my sweetest smile – the one I'd perfected in countless head teachers' offices over the years. "They were just explaining the social hierarchy. Apparently, I'm supposed to grovel at the bottom of it. You know, know my place, kiss the ring, that sort of thing."

"How disappointing for them that you don't seem the grovelling type," he said mildly, though his eyes held something that might have been approval. "Orientation begins in fifteen minutes in the Great Hall. Try not to set anyone on fire before then. The paperwork is a nightmare."

He walked away with the same easy grace he'd arrived with, and I could have sworn I heard him chuckle under his breath.

Victoria's face had turned an interesting shade of red that clashed horribly with her perfect lipstick. "This isn't over, Blackthorne."

"Looking forward to it, Ashford. Maybe next time bring backup that actually talks instead of just flexing and giggling."

Scarlett made a sound like an angry cat. Morgana cracked her knuckles in a way that suggested she was imagining them connecting with my face.

Victoria stalked off with her minions in tow, her heels clicking against the cobblestones in a rhythm that promised trouble.

I stood there alone at the gates for a moment, taking a deep breath of autumn air that smelt like dead leaves and possibility. The weight of what I'd just done – making enemies in my first five minutes – should have worried me more. But honestly? After years of being the weird kid, the foster kid, the kid whose magic manifested in ways that scared everyone including herself, I was tired of trying to fit in.

Ravenwood Academy. Where apparently the mean girls had magic powers and the professors looked like they'd stepped out of my darkest, most inappropriate fantasies.

This was going to be interesting.

Or a complete disaster.

Probably both.

16

Chapter Two

Orientation and Other Forms of Torture

The Great Hall was exactly what you'd expect from a place called the Great Hall – vaulted ceilings that disappeared into shadow, massive chandeliers that floated without chains and swayed gently despite the absence of any breeze, and long tables that looked like they'd witnessed centuries of magical drama, their dark wood scarred with mysterious burns and marks that suggested not all dinner conversations ended peacefully.

About sixty women milled around, ranging in age from early twenties to mid-thirties. Apparently, Ravenwood didn't believe in age limits when it came to magical education. I spotted women with wedding rings, women with crow's feet, women who looked like they'd come straight from corporate jobs. Magic didn't discriminate based on when it decided to manifest strongly enough to warrant formal training.

I found a seat near the back, strategically positioned near both an exit and a window – old habits from a lifetime of needing escape routes. The whispers started before my arse hit the chair.

"That's her – the one who challenged Victoria..."

"...heard she burnt down her entire high school..."

"...killed someone with her magic..."

"...looks like trouble..."

The rumours were already growing. By tomorrow, I'd probably be credited with burning down entire cities and seducing professors in the car park. The truth was always less interesting than the fiction people created.

"Is this seat taken?"

I looked up to find a woman with wild copper curls and magic-stained fingers hovering nearby. She had the kind of smile that suggested she'd rather be anywhere else but was determined to make the best of it. Her dress looked like she'd bought it five minutes ago and hadn't bothered removing the tags – I could see one sticking out from her collar.

"All yours," I said, moving my bag from the adjacent chair.

She plopped down with a sigh of relief that seemed to come from her soul. "Thank God. I was starting to think I'd have to sit with the clone army." She nodded towards the front, where Victoria held court with a group of women who all seemed to shop at the same stores and use the same hair stylist. They moved in sync, like a school of well-dressed fish.

"You mean Victoria's fan club?"

"Is that what we're calling them? I was going with 'the Stepford Witches', but yours is good too." She stuck out a magic-covered hand, not seeming to care that she'd probably leave marks on anything she touched. "Iris Moonwater. I'm repeating my second year because I may have accidentally turned Professor Grimwood into a toad last semester."

I shook her hand, trying not to laugh at the mental image. "Raven Blackthorne. I'm new here, but I've already been marked for death by Queen Victoria."

"Oh, you're the car fire girl! That story's already made the rounds. Did you really trap your ex in a burning vehicle?"

"He had it coming. He cheated on me with my sister."

"Ouch. Yeah, he definitely had it coming. I would have gone for the balls personally, but fire works too." Iris leaned closer, lowering her voice to a conspiratorial whisper. "Fair warning – Victoria doesn't make idle threats. She's got the magical power to back up her mean girl routine. Last year, she cursed a girl so badly, she had to drop out. Nobody could prove it was Victoria, but everyone knew."

"What kind of curse?"

"The girl's magic inverted. Every spell she tried to cast backfired. Light spells created darkness, healing spells caused injuries, transformation spells turned things inside out instead of into something else. It was brutal. They say she's still in therapy, both magical and regular."

Before I could respond, the massive doors at the front of the hall swung open with a boom that silenced every conversation. A woman strode in who could only be the Headmistress. She was tall, severe, with steel-grey hair pulled back in a bun so tight it looked painful and probably gave her a permanent headache. Her robes were black with silver embroidery that seemed to move when you weren't looking directly at it, forming patterns that hurt to follow.

"Welcome to Ravenwood Academy," she said, her voice carrying without amplification, filling every corner of the massive hall. "I am Headmistress Thornbury. You are here because you have demonstrated exceptional magical ability. However, ability without discipline is chaos. Chaos without control is destruction. Over the next three years, we will transform your raw power into refined skill. Those of you who survive the training will emerge as true witches, capable of shaping reality itself."

She paused, letting the word 'survive' sink in.

"Ravenwood has stood for three centuries," she continued, beginning to pace like a general addressing troops. "Our graduates have gone on to shape the magical world. They serve on the High Council, lead covens, advance the boundaries of magical knowledge. But for every success story, there are a dozen failures. Women who couldn't handle the pressure, who let their power consume them, who forgot that magic demands respect and discipline above all else."

She went on about rules, expectations, and consequences. No magic in the dormitories without supervision (yeah, right). No hexing other students (sure, whatever). No summoning demons on school grounds (apparently, this needed to be explicitly stated, which raised questions about previous student activities). No experimenting with time magic without written permission in triplicate. No raising the dead, even small animals. No opening portals to other dimensions, even tiny ones. The list went on.

"Your schedules have been delivered to your rooms via the house brownies," she continued. "Classes begin tomorrow at eight sharp. Tardiness will not be tolerated. Incompetence will not be tolerated. Failure will not be tolerated. Weakness, self-pity, and excuses will definitely not be tolerated."

"Cheerful lady," I muttered under my breath.

Iris snorted, trying to disguise it as a cough. "You should see her when she's actually angry. Legend says she once turned a student into a statue for a week just for interrupting her morning coffee."

"And now," the Headmistress said, her sharp gaze sweeping across the assembled students, "a demonstration from one of our most accomplished students to show you what you might achieve with dedication and proper instruction. Ms Ashford?"

Of course. Of fucking course.

Victoria stood and walked to the centre of the hall with the confidence of someone who'd done this many times before, who'd been waiting for this moment since she woke up. Her heels clicked against the stone floor in perfect rhythm, and she'd somehow touched up her lipstick since our encounter at the gates.

She raised her hands, and the air around her began to shimmer like heat waves off hot asphalt. Slowly, threads of pure golden light emerged from her fingertips, weaving together in intricate patterns that would make a spider jealous. The threads formed shapes – birds that flew in perfect formation around the hall, flowers that bloomed and withered in seconds showing the entire lifecycle of nature, geometric patterns that hurt to look at directly because they seemed to exist in more than three dimensions.

The light birds dove and swooped over our heads, close enough that some students ducked. The flowers released glowing pollen that fell like snow but disappeared before touching anything. It was beautiful, complex, and absolutely designed to make the rest of us feel inadequate.

The display culminated in a phoenix made entirely of light, its wings spanning the width of the hall. Every feather was perfectly detailed, every movement graceful and deliberate. It let out a silent cry – you couldn't hear it, but you could feel it in your bones – before exploding into thousands of golden sparks that rained down on the assembled students like blessing and warning combined.

The applause was thunderous. Victoria curtsied with false modesty that fooled exactly no one, her smile sharp enough to cut.

"Show off," Iris muttered, crossing her arms.

"Can you do that?" I asked, still watching the last golden sparks fade.

"God, no. I can barely manage a light orb without setting something on fire. And don't get me started on my attempt at magical origami – the paper cranes came alive and tried to peck everyone's eyes out. You?"

"I don't do light," I said, flexing my fingers and feeling the fire under my skin respond. "I do fire. Just fire. But I do it very, very well."

"How very on-brand for someone named Blackthorne."

The Headmistress dismissed us with instructions to find our dormitory assignments and a final warning about curfew, proper magical hygiene, and the consequences of unauthorised spell-casting. The crowd filed out slowly, everyone chattering about Victoria's display and the upcoming school year, their voices echoing off the stone walls.

I was almost to the door when someone grabbed my arm. I spun, ready to fight, only to find myself face-to-face with Professor Darkwood. Again. The man had a talent for appearing out of nowhere.

"A word, Ms Blackthorne?"

His hand on my arm was warm, even through my jacket. I nodded, not trusting my voice, and followed him to an alcove away from the crowd. The space was small, intimate, and I could smell his cologne – something woody with an undertone of smoke.

"You're going to have a target on your back," he said without preamble, his voice low enough that I had to lean in to hear him. "Victoria Ashford doesn't like being challenged, and you've publicly embarrassed her. Twice now, if you count the display just now."

"What display? I just sat there…"

"You didn't applaud. You didn't look impressed. For someone like Victoria, that's worse than direct confrontation."

"Are you telling me to apologise? Play nice? Bow down to the queen bee and beg forgiveness?"

"I'm telling you to be careful. And to come to me if things escalate beyond normal school rivalry." His eyes were serious, concerned in a way that seemed personal rather than professional.

"Why do you care?"

He studied me for a moment, and I could have sworn his gaze lingered on my mouth before returning to my eyes. "Let's just say I have a vested interest in keeping promising students from getting themselves expelled. Or worse."

"Worse?"

"Ravenwood has a cemetery for a reason, Ms Blackthorne. Not all magical accidents are survivable. Not all rivalries end with graduation."

The weight of that statement hung between us like a physical thing.

He released my arm and walked away, leaving me standing there with my skin still tingling where he'd touched me and my mind racing with questions I wasn't sure I wanted answered.

Chapter Three

Roommates and Other Punishments

My dorm room was on the third floor of the east tower, which meant climbing approximately eight thousand spiral stairs while hauling my duffel bag. By the time I reached the door marked 313, I was sweating through my formal attire and seriously reconsidering my life choices. The stairs seemed designed to make you suffer, each step slightly different in height, just enough to throw off your rhythm.

The door was already open, held by what looked like a small brass dragon that watched me with ruby eyes as I approached. Inside, I found chaos.

Half the room looked like a gothic cathedral had exploded – black lace draped over everything, silver candlesticks in various states of melting, and what appeared to be an actual human skull on the desk wearing a small top hat. The other half was an explosion of colour – tie-dyed tapestries covering every surface, crystal formations in every shade of the rainbow arranged in complex patterns, and enough plants to start a small jungle. Some of the plants were definitely not native to this dimension.

In the middle of this decorative war zone stood two women, glaring at each other with the intensity of sworn enemies forced to share a space.

"I told you, the altar stays," said the one dressed like she'd raided Morticia Addams' closet and added her own flair with silver jewellery that probably doubled as weapons.

"And I told you, I need that space for my herb garden," countered the other, who looked like she'd just returned from Woodstock by way of a crystal shop explosion. "Plants need natural light, and that's the only window that gets morning sun."

They both turned when I entered, their argument momentarily forgotten.

"You must be the third roommate," gothic girl said, looking me up and down with an appraising eye. "I'm Lilith. And before you ask, yes, it's my real name. My parents had a sense of humour."

"Moon," said the hippie, though she said it like it should be spelled with extra o's and possibly some cosmic significance. "Like, cosmic Moon, not regular moon. My parents were having a spiritual phase when I was born."

"Raven," I said, dropping my bag on the unclaimed bed with relief. The mattress was thin, the frame creaked ominously, but it was mine. "So what's this about an altar?"

"Lilith wants to set up a death altar in the common area," Moon explained, gesturing wildly with hands covered in henna tattoos. "But that's where my healing crystals need to go. They require eastern exposure for proper energy alignment, and the vibes from a death altar would totally throw off their frequencies."

"It's not a death altar," Lilith protested, adjusting one of her many necklaces – this one appeared to be made of tiny bones. "It's for communing with spirits. Completely different thing. Death altars are for necromancy. Spirit altars are for communication. Totally different magical schools."

"Dead spirits," Moon pointed out, not unreasonably.

"Well, yes, the living ones don't usually need summoning. They're already here. Walking around. Being alive."

I looked between them, then at the disputed space – a small area by the window that both clearly coveted like it was the last piece of chocolate in existence.

"Rock, paper, scissors," I said.

They stared at me like I'd suggested we solve this with interpretive dance.

"Best two out of three. Winner gets the space. Loser shuts up about it."

"That's... actually not a bad idea," Lilith admitted, putting down what looked like a ceremonial dagger she'd been using as a letter opener.

Three minutes later, Moon was victorious and already arranging crystals while humming something that sounded like whale songs. Lilith sullenly moved her skull to her desk, muttering about the cosmic unfairness of random chance.

"So," I said, unpacking my meagre belongings – three changes of clothes, a toothbrush that had seen better days, and a photo of my last foster family's dog (the only family member I'd actually liked), "what's the deal with this place? Besides the obvious mean girls and mysterious professors?"

"Oh, you've met Victoria already?" Lilith perked up, apparently distracted from her loss. "She's the worst. Acts like her family funding half the academy makes her royalty. Which, technically, in the magical world, it kind of does."

"They really fund half?"

"Her grandmother was Evangeline Ashford," Moon said, like that should mean something.

When she saw my blank look, she gasped dramatically. "You don't know who Evangeline Ashford was? She literally wrote the book on modern light magic. 'Illumination and Illusion: A Practitioner's Guide'? It's required reading for second years. Revolutionary theories on the relationship between light and consciousness?"

"I'm more of a burn-things-down kind of witch," I said, demonstrating by creating a small flame above my palm. It danced there, eager and hungry.

"Clearly," Moon said, eyeing the flame with the wariness of someone who'd had bad experiences with fire. "That's actually impressive control for someone untrained. Most pyrokinetics can't maintain a flame that small without it either dying or exploding."

"It's not about control," I said, making the flame dance between my fingers. "It's about understanding. Fire isn't a tool. It's alive. It wants things. You have to negotiate, not command."

"That's... actually kind of profound," Lilith said, now watching the flame with interest.

"Most people treat elemental magic like it's just energy to be shaped."

Before we could continue the philosophical discussion of magical theory, a knock at the door interrupted us. Iris stood in the doorway, looking frazzled and holding what appeared to be a stack of papers that were actively trying to escape her grasp.

"Raven! Thank God I found you. We have a problem."

"How do we already have a problem?"

"Victoria's called a Circle."

Lilith swore creatively in what sounded like Latin. Moon's crystals actually dimmed, which I didn't know was possible.

"What's a Circle?" I asked, though the ominous reactions suggested I wouldn't like the answer.

"It's technically a traditional gathering for witches to share power and knowledge," Iris explained, wrestling with the papers that seemed determined to flutter away. "But here at Ravenwood, it's more like a magical hazing ritual. Victoria calls them to put people in their place. Publicly. Painfully."

"And let me guess – I'm the guest of honour?"

"Bingo. Midnight, in the old greenhouse behind the academy. And before you ask, no, you can't skip it. If you don't show, Victoria wins by default, and everyone will know you're scared of her. Your reputation will be destroyed before you even have one."

"I'm not scared of some privileged princess with a light-up magic trick."

"That's the spirit," Lilith said, grinning in a way that showed too many teeth. "You'll need it. The last person Victoria called a Circle on ended up in the infirmary for a week. They say she still twitches when she sees bright lights."

"What happened to them?"

"Victoria happened. She challenged them to a magical duel and then proceeded to humiliate them so thoroughly they transferred schools the next day. Didn't even pack their things, just left."

"And the professors allow this?"

"Technically, Circles are part of academic tradition," Moon said, absently adjusting her crystals which were now pulsing with nervous energy. "As long as no one dies or suffers permanent damage, the administration looks the other way. It's supposed to build character or some bullshit."

"No one dies. How reassuring."

"You could always apologise," Iris suggested half-heartedly, though her expression said she knew that was about as likely as me sprouting wings. "Grovel a little. Maybe she'll call it off."

"Have you met me? I don't grovel. I barely even kneel, and that's only to tie my shoes."

"Then you'd better be as good with that fire magic as the rumours suggest," Lilith said, suddenly serious. "Because Victoria's been training since she was five. She knows spells most graduates haven't even heard of. Her family has a private library of magical texts that aren't even in the academy's collection."

I stood tall, testing the weight of the power inside me. It responded eagerly, flames dancing under my skin, begging to be released. The familiar burn filled me with confidence – maybe false confidence, but confidence nonetheless.

"Good thing I don't fight fair."

"You're going to need more than attitude," Moon said, moving to her trunk and pulling out various crystals. "Take these. Protection, strength, clarity."

"I don't really do the crystal thing..."

"Just take them," she insisted, pressing them into my hands. "Even if you don't believe in them, I do, and intention is half of magic."

Lilith moved to her desk, returning with a small vial of something dark. "Graveyard dirt. Blessed under a new moon. Put it in your pocket. It won't help in a fight, but it might make you harder to curse."

"You guys just met me," I said, touched despite myself. "Why are you helping?"

"Because," Iris said, finally getting her papers under control, "anyone who pisses off Victoria Ashford on their first day is our kind of people."

"Plus," Lilith added with a grin, "we really want to see if you can actually beat her. The betting pool is already up to two hundred pounds."

"There's a betting pool?"

"Oh yeah. You're currently at ten-to-one odds against."

"Those are terrible odds."

"Want us to put twenty on you?" Moon asked. "If you win, we'll split the profits."

"Make it fifty," I said, heading for the door. "If I'm going to get my arse kicked, might as well make it profitable."

Chapter Four

Midnight Circles and Bad Decisions

The greenhouse was exactly the kind of place you'd expect to host sketchy midnight magical duels – broken glass panels let in streams of moonlight that cut through the darkness like silver knives, dead vines created shadowy corners perfect for ambushes, and the whole place smelt like rotting vegetation and bad decisions. The structure itself groaned in the wind, as if protesting its use for such purposes.

Victoria was already there when I arrived, surrounded by her usual crowd plus about twenty other students who'd come to watch the show. She'd changed out of her school clothes into something that looked like combat gear designed by a fashion magazine – black leather leggings, a corseted top that was both practical and deliberately intimidating, and boots that could probably kill someone without magic. Her hair was pulled back in a perfect ponytail that wouldn't dare to frizz.

The assembled crowd formed a rough circle, their faces lit by various magical lights – some held orbs of soft blue, others had conjured small floating flames, and one ambitious soul had created what looked like a miniature aurora borealis above her head.

"I wasn't sure you'd show," Victoria said as I approached, her voice carrying easily across the space.

"And miss all this drama? Please. I live for making terrible decisions at midnight in abandoned buildings."

A few people in the crowd chuckled, quickly silencing themselves when Victoria's gaze swept over them.

"You should know," Victoria said, loud enough for everyone to hear, raising her voice like she was giving a presentation, "that Circles have rules. Ancient rules, established when this academy was founded. We each get three spells. No death curses, no permanent maiming, no soul magic. First one who yields or can't continue loses."

"And if I win?"

She laughed. Actually laughed, the sound bright and sharp as broken glass. "You won't. But hypothetically, if you somehow managed to beat me, I'd acknowledge you as an equal. No more harassment, no more problems. You'd have earned your place here."

"And if you win?"

"You leave Ravenwood. Tonight. Pack your little bag and never come back."

The crowd murmured. That was a steep price. Some people were already pulling out money, adjusting their bets.

"Deal," I said without hesitation.

More murmurs, some gasps. Iris, who'd come to support me along with my roommates, looked like she might faint. Moon was clutching her crystals so hard her knuckles were white. Lilith, at least, was grinning like this was the best entertainment she'd had in years.

"Excellent." Victoria stepped back, creating space between us. The crowd moved too, widening the circle. "Would someone like to officiate? We need a witness to make this binding."

"I will."

Professor Darkwood emerged from the shadows, because of course he did. The man had a talent for dramatic entrances that would make a theatre graduate jealous. He was dressed in all black, making him almost invisible until he wanted to be seen.

"Professor," Victoria said, and was that nervousness in her voice? "I didn't expect..."

"A Circle requires an official witness to be binding," he said smoothly. "Unless you'd prefer to make this an unsanctioned brawl? I'm sure the Headmistress would be very interested to hear about unsanctioned magical duelling."

"No, of course not. We follow the rules here."

His eyes found mine, and something in them made my stomach flip. "Ms Blackthorne, are you certain you want to do this? The stakes are quite high."

"Absolutely."

"Very well." He positioned himself between us, his presence somehow making the space feel smaller and more dangerous. "Standard Circle rules apply. Three spells each, no killing, no permanent damage. The Circle ends when one witch yields or cannot continue. Begin on my signal."

He stepped back, his movement fluid as water. The crowd held its breath.

"Begin."

Victoria moved first, her hands already glowing with that golden light she'd displayed earlier. She sent it towards me in a wave, and I could feel the spell's intent – it was meant to bind, to wrap me in chains of light that would hold me helpless. The magic tasted of superiority and cruel amusement.

I didn't try to dodge. Instead, I let my fire roar to life, meeting her light with a wall of flames that shot up from the ground. The two forces collided in the centre of the greenhouse, sending sparks both gold and red cascading around us like the world's most dangerous fireworks display. The heat was intense enough that people in the front row stepped back.

"Brute force?" Victoria laughed, already preparing her next attack. "How predictable. How... common."

She changed tactics, her second spell more subtle. The light condensed into needles, hundreds of them, flying at me from every direction. They whistled through the air, each one aimed at a pressure point.

I dropped to one knee, slamming my palm against the ground. Fire erupted in a circle around me, a tornado of flames that incinerated the light needles before they could reach me. But Victoria was already moving, using my defensive position to her advantage.

Her third spell was beautiful and terrible. The light formed into a massive serpent, scales glittering like diamonds, each one reflecting the moon and the magical lights of the watching crowd. The construct was at least twenty feet long, and it moved with sinuous grace that shouldn't have been possible for something made of pure energy. This was advanced magic, the kind that required not just power but incredible control and years of practice.

The serpent reared back, its hood spreading like a cobra's, and I could see fangs made of concentrated light that would burn as surely as any flame. It struck, moving faster than any living snake, and I barely rolled out of the way. The ground where I'd been standing sizzled, leaving a charred mark in the shape of the serpent's jaw.

It came at me again, jaws wide, and I knew I couldn't keep dodging. Victoria was grinning, already tasting victory, her supporters in the crowd starting to cheer.

So I did something stupid. Gloriously, recklessly stupid.

Instead of fighting the serpent, I dove straight into its mouth.

The crowd screamed. Victoria's eyes widened in shock. Even Professor Darkwood stepped forward as if to intervene. But I wasn't suicidal – I was strategic. And maybe a little crazy, but that was beside the point.

Light magic, for all its beauty and power, had one weakness: it was still just energy. And energy could be consumed, transformed, repurposed. Fire didn't just destroy – it transmuted.

I let my fire explode outward from inside the serpent, not trying to destroy it but to absorb it, to feed on it. Fire needed fuel, and Victoria had just given me a feast of pure magical energy. The sensation was overwhelming – like drinking lightning, like swallowing the sun.

The serpent imploded in a cascade of golden sparks, its light rushing into me, and for a moment I thought I might actually explode from the power. My skin glowed from within, my eyes burned like stars, and when I opened my mouth, smoke poured out like dragon's breath.

"My turn," I said, and my voice was layered with heat and power, echoing with the crackle of flames.

My first spell was simple – a fireball the size of a basketball that I hurled at Victoria's feet. She danced back, light shields springing up instinctively, but the fire wasn't meant to hit her. It was meant to blind her, to fill her vision with spots of brightness that would make her next move predictable.

While she was dealing with the explosion and the shower of sparks, I sent my second spell – a low wave of fire that raced across the ground like liquid, turning the dead vines into burning whips that reached for her ankles with grasping fingers of flame. The vines came alive with fire, writhing and seeking.

She levitated to avoid them, which was exactly what I wanted. In the air, she had no leverage, no way to dodge what came next.

My third spell had been building since the moment I absorbed her serpent. I released it all at once – not as fire, but as pure heat. The air around Victoria superheated instantly, making it impossible to breathe, impossible to think. The very molecules of air burned without flame. Her light shields couldn't block what was already inside them, what surrounded them, what was everywhere and nowhere at once.

She held on for longer than I expected, her magic flaring desperately, trying to create a bubble of cool air, trying to push back the heat. But eventually, inevitably, she dropped to her knees, gasping for breath that wouldn't come.

"Yield," she croaked, the word barely audible.

The heat dissipated instantly. I stood there, steam rising from my skin like I was a volcano that had just finished erupting, watching as Victoria's friends rushed to help her up. Scarlett produced a vial of something blue that she helped Victoria drink, while Morgana glared at me with undisguised hatred.

"The Circle is concluded," Professor Darkwood announced, his voice cutting through the shocked silence. "Ms Blackthorne is victorious."

The greenhouse was silent for a heartbeat. Then Iris let out a whoop that started a chain reaction of excited chatter. Money changed hands rapidly, and I noticed Lilith collecting what looked like a substantial sum from several very unhappy-looking third years.

Victoria looked at me with something between hatred and respect, still breathing heavily. "That was... impossible. You shouldn't have been able to absorb my construct. That's master-level transmutation."

"I fight to win."

She straightened, pulling away from Scarlett's supporting arm with a wince. "A deal's a deal. You're... an equal. No more problems from me."

"Glad to hear it."

She turned to leave, then paused, looking back over her shoulder. "But Blackthorne? This isn't over. Not by a long shot. Being equals doesn't mean we're friends."

"Wouldn't dream of it, Ashford."

She left with her entourage, and suddenly I was surrounded by other students, all talking at once, asking questions, some even asking for autographs on various items – notebooks, arms, one ambitious girl wanted me to sign her grimoire.

"That was insane!" Lilith appeared at my elbow, clutching a substantial roll of cash. "You literally ate her spell! We're rich!"

"How did you know that would work?" Moon asked, her crystals now glowing with excited energy.

"I didn't," I admitted, suddenly feeling the exhaustion hit me like a truck. "It was a calculated risk. Or maybe an uncalculated risk. Either way, it worked."

"That was idiotic," a familiar voice said. The crowd parted for Professor Darkwood like he was Moses and they were the Red Sea. "Absorbing another witch's construct could have killed you. Or worse, corrupted your own magic permanently. You could have become a magical null, or had your power inverted, or simply exploded."

"But it didn't."

"Through sheer luck." He stepped closer, and I caught that scent again – sandalwood and something darker, like smoke from a wood that shouldn't be burnt. "You have raw power, Ms Blackthorne, but power without control is..."

"Chaos. Yeah, I got the speech from the Headmistress. Twice, actually."

His jaw tightened, a muscle jumping there that I found oddly fascinating. "Report to my office tomorrow after your regular classes. If you're going to take risks like that, you need proper training before you kill yourself or someone else."

"Is that a punishment or a reward?"

His eyes darkened to the colour of storm clouds at midnight. "That depends entirely on you and how seriously you take this. Magic isn't a game, Ms Blackthorne."

"Could have fooled me, with all the formal rules and spectators."

He walked away without another word, leaving me standing there with my skin still humming from residual magic and something else – something that had nothing to do with the duel and everything to do with the way he'd looked at me, like I was a problem he wanted to solve and a temptation he wanted to avoid.

"Girl," Iris said, counting her share of the winnings, "you either have the best luck or the worst luck I've ever seen."

"What do you mean?"

"You just made an enemy-turned-reluctant-ally of the most powerful student in school and caught the attention of the most dangerous professor on campus. That's either going to end very well or very, very badly."

Looking around at the mix of awed and calculating faces, the way some students stepped back when I looked at them while others seemed to lean in, I had a feeling she was right.

"Come on," Moon said, linking her arm through mine. "Let's get you back to the dorm before you collapse. You're shaking."

She was right. Now that the adrenaline was fading, I could feel the tremors running through my body. Using that much magic, especially in such an uncontrolled way, had taken more out of me than I wanted to admit.

As we walked back through the darkness, Lilith chattering excitedly about odds and profits, Moon humming something soothing, and Iris planning celebration drinks, I couldn't shake the feeling that I'd just changed something fundamental about my time at Ravenwood.

Whether that change was for better or worse remained to be seen.

Chapter Five

Private Lessons and Dangerous Games

My first week of actual classes was a special kind of hell that made me nostalgic for regular high school, where the worst thing that could happen was detention or a pop quiz.

Potions with Professor Grimwood (who kept giving me suspicious looks like she expected me to turn her into a toad like Iris had, and had taken to keeping a mirror on her desk to check her appearance every few minutes). The classroom reeked of sulphur and something sweet that made my teeth ache, and my first attempt at a simple healing potion had somehow turned into something that dissolved the pewter cauldron.

Divination with Professor Moonwhisper (who predicted I would "face great trials and greater temptations" while staring meaningfully at her crystal ball, which just looked like a glorified snow globe to me). She spent half the class talking about the importance of "opening your third eye" and the other half complaining that the cosmic vibrations were off because someone had used magic to cheat on their homework.

Magical Theory with Professor Ashwood, who happened to be Victoria's aunt and made no secret of her displeasure at my continued existence at Ravenwood. She had Victoria's same perfect bone structure but none of her niece's charm – every word out of her mouth dripped with disdain, especially when addressing me.

"Ms Blackthorne," she'd said on my first day, "I trust you understand that raw power without theoretical foundation is like giving a child a loaded weapon."

"I understand perfectly, Professor," I'd replied sweetly. "Though I'd argue it's more like giving a teenager a flamethrower – much more fun and only slightly more likely to end in property damage."

The class had laughed. She had not.

But it was Thursday afternoon, standing outside Professor Darkwood's office, that had my nerves actually showing themselves. The heavy oak door seemed to loom over me, carved with symbols that shifted when you weren't looking directly at them.

"Enter," his voice called before I could knock.

Show-off.

His office was exactly what you'd expect from a professor of Defensive Magic – dark wood that seemed to absorb light, leather-bound books that looked older than the academy itself, and weapons on the walls that looked both ancient and deadly. There was a glass case containing what appeared to be a human hand made of silver, still wearing rings. I decided not to ask.

He sat behind a massive desk that could have doubled as a small boat, reviewing papers with the kind of intensity usually reserved for defusing bombs. The afternoon light from the tall window behind him created a halo effect that would have been angelic if not for the fact that everything else about him suggested danger.

He didn't look up when I entered, just gestured to a chair.

"Sit."

I sat, trying not to fidget like a student called to the head teacher's office. Though technically, that's kind of what this was.

He continued reading for another minute, and I got the distinct impression he was making me wait on purpose. Power play. I could respect that, even as it annoyed me.

Finally, he set the papers aside and looked at me. In the afternoon light streaming through his window, his eyes were more silver than grey, like mercury given form.

"Do you know why you won that duel with Ms Ashford?"

"Because I was better?"

"No. You won because you were unpredictable. Victoria has trained her entire life in traditional magic. She knows a thousand spells and can execute them flawlessly. You know perhaps a dozen spells, poorly, but you use them in ways no classically trained witch would expect."

"So I'm creatively incompetent. Great. That's exactly what every girl wants to hear."

His lips twitched in what might have been amusement. "In a way, yes. But that creativity won't save you forever. Eventually, you'll face someone who can match your unpredictability with sheer skill, and you'll lose. Badly. Possibly fatally."

"Hence the private lessons?"

"Hence the private lessons." He stood, moving around the desk with that fluid grace that suggested he'd had combat training beyond just magic. "Your fire magic is powerful but unrefined. You use it like a club when it could be a scalpel. Stand up."

I stood, very aware of how close he was now. This near, I could see that the scar through his eyebrow extended slightly onto his temple, and there were flecks of gold in those silver eyes.

"Show me your fire. Just a small flame."

I held out my hand, conjuring a flame the size of a candle. Easy. Child's play. I'd been doing this since I was thirteen and accidentally set my foster parents' curtains on fire during an argument.

"Now make it blue."

"What?"

"Blue fire burns hotter than orange. Change the temperature without changing the size."

I concentrated, trying to push more heat into the flame. It flickered, sputtered, grew larger, then died completely.

"Again."

I tried again. Failed again. The flame either grew to bonfire size or extinguished entirely.

"You're trying to force it," he said, moving behind me. "Fire isn't just destruction. It's transformation. Feel the energy, don't command it."

He placed his hands on my shoulders, and I nearly jumped out of my skin. His touch was warm, firm, and sent electricity down my spine that had nothing to do with magic.

"Relax," he said, his voice low enough to make me shiver. "Close your eyes."

I closed them, hyper-aware of his hands on me, the warmth of his body behind mine, the way his breath stirred the hair at the nape of my neck.

"Feel your power," he said. "Don't think about it, just feel it. Let it flow like water, not explode like dynamite."

His hands moved down my arms, guiding them into position. Every nerve ending was on fire, and not from magic. This was something else, something that made my heart race and my breath catch.

"Open your eyes."

I did. A perfect blue flame danced in my palm, steady and controlled, so hot it made the air shimmer but so controlled it didn't even warm my skin.

"Excellent," he said, but he didn't move away.

I could feel the solid warmth of him behind me, close enough that if I leaned back slightly... "You have potential, Ms Blackthorne. Raw, dangerous, magnificent potential."

"Is that why you offered to train me? Because of my potential?"

He was quiet for a moment, and I could feel his breath on my neck, warm and measured. "Perhaps."

"Or perhaps you have other reasons?"

He stepped back abruptly, the loss of his warmth almost painful. The blue flame flickered and died.

"That's enough for today. Same time next week."

"That's it? Ten minutes and we're done?"

"Unless you'd prefer to continue?" There was something in his voice, a challenge maybe, or an invitation. The kind of tone that suggested we both knew we weren't just talking about magic lessons.

"I could handle more."

His eyes darkened to storm-cloud grey. "I'm sure you could. But we'll take this slowly. You're not the only one who needs to maintain control."

The weight of that statement hung between us like a physical thing, heavy with implication.

"Is this about what Scarlett said? About you getting too invested in certain students?"

"Scarlett says many things, not all of them true."

"But some of them are?"

He moved back to his desk, putting distance between us like it was a shield. "What happened between Scarlett and myself is not your concern."

"You were involved with her?"

"No. She wanted to be involved. I declined. She didn't handle rejection well." He picked up his pen, spinning it between his fingers in what looked like a nervous habit. "She was brilliant, powerful, but she wanted things I couldn't give her."

"Like what?"

"Things that would have been inappropriate given our positions."

"And now she warns other students away from you?"

"As I said, not your concern." He picked up his papers again, a clear dismissal. "Focus on your studies, Ms Blackthorne. And try not to absorb any more constructs. I'd prefer my students survive the semester."

I headed for the door, then paused, my hand on the handle. "For what it's worth, I don't scare easily. Not from Victoria, not from Scarlett, and not from whatever this is between us."

"There is no 'us', Ms Blackthorne."

"Right. Of course not. That's why you can't stop staring at my mouth when you think I'm not looking. That's why your hands lingered on my arms. That's why your voice dropped an octave when you called my potential 'magnificent.'"

I left before he could respond, but not before I caught the flash of heat in his eyes that had nothing to do with magic and everything to do with want.

Chapter Six

Party Crasher

"You have to come," Iris insisted for the fifth time that night, lying upside down on my bed with her feet against the wall. "It's the Autumn Equinox party. Everyone will be there. Even the professors sometimes make appearances, though they pretend they're just checking for violations."

Apparently Ravenwood had a tradition of throwing massive parties for every magical holiday, astronomical event, or day ending in 'y' that students could use as an excuse. This one was being held in the abandoned west tower, which had supposedly been off-limits since a summoning gone wrong in the '80s.

"I don't do parties," I said, not looking up from my Potions textbook, which was actively trying to flip its own pages to more interesting chapters.

"You don't do anything except study and have weird sexual tension with Professor Darkwood during your private lessons," Lilith pointed out from where she was painting her nails black with what smelt suspiciously like actual tar.

"There's no sexual tension."

"Please," Moon said, not even looking up from her tarot spread. "I can feel it from here, and I'm not even in the room when you two are together. The energy signatures are off the charts. The cards literally heat up when I do readings about you two."

"You can't read energy signatures from..."

"Party. Tonight. You're coming." Iris flipped right-side up with surprising agility. "Besides, I heard Victoria's planning something. You should probably be there."

That got my attention. I closed the textbook, which seemed relieved. "Planning what?"

"No idea, but Morgana was gathering some pretty specific ingredients from the advanced potions lab. The kind you'd use for a major enchantment. Or a curse. Or something equally concerning that starts with 'C' and ends with 'atastrophe'."

Despite our "truce", Victoria and I had maintained a careful distance. We didn't hex each other in the halls, but we weren't exactly braiding each other's hair either. She'd stopped actively trying to make my life hell, but there was something in her eyes whenever our paths crossed – a promise that this wasn't over, just postponed.

"Fine. One hour."

"Yes!" Iris actually clapped. "Wear something hot."

"I don't own anything hot. Unless you count the cardigan I accidentally set on fire last week."

"That's what roommates are for," Lilith said, already rifling through her closet with the enthusiasm of someone who'd been waiting for this moment.

An hour later, I stood in the west tower wearing a black dress that belonged to Lilith (and probably violated several decency laws), heels that belonged to Moon (and definitely violated several laws of physics), and more eyeliner than I'd worn in my entire life combined.

The party was already in full swing – someone had enchanted orbs of coloured light to float through the air like drunken fireflies, music pounded from speakers that shouldn't work in a building this old, and the smell of alcohol mixed with various magical herbs filled the air. Some of the herbs were definitely not legal – magical or otherwise.

"Drink?" A guy appeared at my elbow with a red solo cup that was somehow both the most normal and most out of place thing here.

"Pass." I didn't trust drinks I hadn't poured myself, especially not here where someone could literally enchant the liquid to make you do anything.

I spotted Victoria across the room, holding court as usual. She caught my eye and raised her glass in a mock toast. I returned the gesture with my middle finger. Some truces were more fragile than others.

"Didn't expect to see you here."

I turned to find Scarlett, looking unfairly gorgeous in a green dress that matched her eyes and probably cost more than my entire education. Her red hair was styled in vintage waves that belonged in a 1940s movie.

"Didn't expect to be here," I admitted. "But apparently it's a cardinal sin to miss the Equinox party."

"First one's always the wildest. People trying to establish their reputations for the year." She sipped her drink, studying me over the rim with calculating eyes. "Though you've already done that pretty thoroughly. The girl who ate Victoria's light serpent. That's what they're calling you."

"Catchy."

"Among other things. They're also calling you Damien's new pet project."

"We're on a first-name basis with the professors now?"

She laughed, but it wasn't particularly friendly. It was the laugh of someone who knew things you didn't and enjoyed the power that gave them. "Oh, honey. Damien Darkwood and I go way back. We were together for two years before I came to Ravenwood."

That was news that hit like cold water. "He failed to mention that."

"I bet he did. He also probably told you I couldn't handle rejection?"

"Something like that."

"Here's what actually happened," she said, moving closer, her voice dropping to a conversational tone that was somehow more threatening than shouting. "Damien likes powerful witches. The more dangerous, the better. He collects them, trains them, seduces them, and then moves on when someone more interesting comes along. I was his favourite until a pyrokinetic named Amber showed up. Sound familiar?"

"What happened to Amber?"

"She dropped out. Couldn't handle it when he moved on to the next girl. The one after that transferred schools. The one after that…" She shrugged, taking another sip. "Well, let's just say the cemetery isn't just for show."

"You're lying."

"Am I? Ask him about Sophia Colman. See how quickly he changes the subject."

Before I could respond, the lights suddenly dimmed to almost nothing, leaving us in near darkness except for the floating orbs which seemed to pulse in response to something.

Victoria stood in the centre of the room, her hands glowing with that familiar golden light that seemed brighter in the darkness.

"Ladies and gentlemen," she announced, her voice carrying easily over the music which had stopped as if on cue, "in honour of the Equinox, I've prepared something special. A little game, you might say."

The light from her hands spread out, forming a perfect circle on the floor. Runes appeared in the air, floating and spinning, writing themselves in languages that hurt to look at directly.

"Truth or Dare, magical style. Anyone who steps in the circle has to play. The magic will know if you're lying or if you refuse a dare. The consequences..." She smiled, and in the strange light, it looked almost predatory. "Well, that would spoil the fun, wouldn't it?"

People immediately started backing away from the circle, but drunk student witches are nothing if not predictable. Within minutes, someone had shoved someone else into the circle as a joke, and the game began.

It started harmlessly enough. Minor truths about crushes and homework ("Yes, I copied Sarah's Transfiguration essay"), dares to levitate objects or transform drinks into different colours. One girl admitted to having a crush on Professor Moonwhisper, which caused quite a stir.

Then Victoria's eyes found mine across the room.

"Raven," she called out, her voice honey-sweet poison. "Don't be shy."

"I'm good, thanks. I don't play games with magical compulsion."

"What's wrong? Scared of a little truth? Or are you afraid of what you might be dared to do?"

The crowd started chanting. "Circle! Circle! Circle!"

I could have walked away. Should have walked away. But I've never been good at backing down from a challenge, especially not when the entire school was watching.

I stepped into the circle.

The magic hit immediately, like invisible chains wrapping around me, sinking into my skin, my bones, my very soul. Not painful, but definitely present. A compulsion to play, to follow the rules, to tell the truth or complete the dare. It felt like having someone else's will imposed over your own, and every fibre of my being wanted to rebel against it.

"Excellent," Victoria purred. "Truth or dare?"

"Truth."

"Is it true that you've been having private lessons with Professor Darkwood? Alone? In his office? With the door locked?"

The crowd went silent. This was dangerous territory – professor-student relationships were strictly forbidden, grounds for immediate expulsion for the student and termination for the professor.

The magic compelled me to answer, the words pulling themselves from my throat.

"Yes," I said, because the magic wouldn't let me lie. "He's teaching me control. My magic is too volatile without proper training."

"Just control?" Victoria's smile was vicious. "Nothing else? No lingering touches? No heated looks? No inappropriate tension?"

"That's four questions, not one. But nice try."

"Fine. My turn's over." She looked around the crowd, her eyes searching. "Who's next?"

Scarlett stepped forward like this had been planned all along. "I'll go. Raven, truth or dare?"

I should have known they were working together. The smart thing would be to pick truth again, but the magic of the circle had its own momentum, and I could feel it pushing me towards the more dangerous choice.

"Dare."

"I dare you to summon Professor Darkwood here. Right now. Using whatever means necessary."

"That's not..."

"The magic says it's possible," Scarlett interrupted, and she was right. I could feel the circle's magic confirming it. "Which means you can do it. Unless you want to face the consequences of refusing?"

The circle pulsed, and I felt a sharp pain in my chest, like someone had reached in and squeezed my heart. A warning. The consequences would be bad. Really bad. The kind of bad that might be permanent.

"Fine."

I closed my eyes, reaching for my fire. But instead of releasing it in its usual destructive form, I sent it out like a signal flare, a beacon of pure magical energy that anyone with sensitivity would feel. It was dangerous – sending out that much raw power was like screaming in a library full of predators – but I hoped Professor Darkwood would recognise my magical signature and understand.

It was a long shot, but...

"What an interesting party."

Everyone spun around. Professor Darkwood stood in the doorway, looking lethal in all black, his expression unreadable. The temperature in the room seemed to drop ten degrees.

"Professor," Victoria said, recovering first. "We were just..."

"Playing with binding circles and compulsion magic?" He stepped into the room, the crowd parted. "Both of which are illegal without supervision. Both of which carry potential sentences of magical binding. Both of which I'm sure you knew when you cast them."

His eyes found mine, still trapped in the circle. Something flickered in them – anger? Concern? Something deeper?

"Release her," he said quietly, but his voice carried the kind of authority that made you want to obey immediately.

"She has to finish the game," Victoria said, though she looked less certain now. "Those are the rules. The magic demands completion."

"Then let's finish it." He stepped into the circle himself, and the crowd gasped. A professor entering a student's truth or dare circle was unprecedented. "Ms Blackthorne, truth or dare?"

I stared at him. He was giving me an out, but at what cost? What would this mean for him?

"Truth."

"Have you ever wanted to burn this whole place down? Every stone, every rule, every tradition that makes this place what it is?"

The question was so unexpected, I laughed. The magic compelled honesty, but this was easy. "Only every other day. The other days I just want to burn down specific parts. Like the Potions classroom after I melted another cauldron."

"Understandable." He turned to Victoria, and there was something dangerous in his expression. "The game is finished. Release the circle. Now."

"That's not how..."

"Release it, or I'll break it myself and let the backlash hit whoever cast it." His power flared, shadows dancing on the walls despite the magical lights. "Your choice, Ms Ashford."

Victoria's face went pale. A broken binding circle would rebound on its creator with triple the force, possibly causing permanent magical damage. She quickly dispelled the magic, the runes dissolving like smoke.

I stumbled as the compulsion released, my knees suddenly weak. Professor Darkwood – Damien – caught my arm, steadying me.

"You ok?"

"Fine. Just... intense."

"My office. Now."

"But..."

"That wasn't a request."

He strode out, clearly expecting me to follow. I looked at Iris, who made shooing motions, then at Victoria and Scarlett, who were both watching with calculating expressions, like predators who'd just seen prey reveal a weakness.

This night had officially gone to hell.

And something told me it was about to get worse.

Chapter Seven

Lines Crossed

His office was dark except for the fireplace, which roared to life the moment we entered, casting dancing shadows on the walls. Damien went straight to a cabinet I hadn't noticed before, pulling out a bottle of amber liquid and two glasses.

"Drink," he said, handing me one.

"I don't..."

"It's medicinal. Binding circles leave residual effects – magical contamination that can linger for days if not treated. This will help."

I took a sip and immediately coughed. It burned like liquid fire, but in a good way, clearing my head and making my magic settle.

"What the hell were you thinking?" he asked, sitting on the edge of his desk instead of behind it, a casual position that somehow made him seem more dangerous.

"I was thinking it was just a stupid party game."

"There's no such thing as 'just' anything when magic is involved. Victoria could have used that circle to make you do anything. Anything. Reveal your deepest secrets, humiliate yourself, harm yourself. The compulsion magic in that circle was strong enough to override basic self-preservation."

"She wouldn't..."

"She would. She has before." He drained his glass in one motion. "Three years ago, she used a similar circle to make a girl confess every secret she had. Every embarrassing thought, every private moment, every shameful desire. The humiliation was so complete, the girl tried to erase her own memories. The spell went wrong. She's still in the psychiatric ward at St Bartholomew's, convinced she's living in a different reality where none of it happened."

"Jesus."

"Victoria plays for keeps, Raven. I warned you about making enemies."

"Yeah, well, she started it."

He laughed, short and harsh. "You sound like a child."

"And you sound like you care more than a professor should."

The words hung between us, heavy and dangerous. He set down his glass with deliberate care, standing to pace to the window that overlooked the dark grounds.

"Scarlett talked to you."

"She mentioned some things. Amber. Sophia Colman. Your apparent pattern of collecting dangerous witches."

His shoulders tensed. "Sophia was a mistake."

"Because she died?"

He turned, his face half in shadow, half lit by firelight. "Because I let feelings cloud my judgment. She was brilliant, powerful, reckless. I thought I could help her, train her, keep her safe. I thought I could maintain professional boundaries while still…"

"While still what?"

"While still caring about her more than I should have."

"What happened?"

"She went too far. Tried to absorb energy from a ley line without proper preparation. The ley lines that run under Ravenwood are ancient, powerful, and hungry. They don't give power – they take it. I found her too late. She was empty, just a shell. Her body lived for three more days, but Sophia was gone."

"And you blamed yourself."

"I was her teacher. Her mentor. Her…" He stopped, running a hand through his hair.

"Her lover?"

"No. Never that. I maintained that boundary, at least. But she wanted more, and when I refused…" He turned back to the window. "She took the risk to prove she was powerful enough for me. To make me see her as an equal. She thought if she could master a ley line, I'd have no reason to keep her at a distance."

"That's not your fault."

"Isn't it? I saw the signs. The growing recklessness, the need to impress, the way she looked at me like I was salvation and damnation combined. I should have distanced myself completely. Should have transferred her to another professor. Should have done a dozen things differently."

"Is that why you're keeping me at arm's length? You see the same patterns?"

"I see similarities," he admitted. "The power, the defiance, the complete lack of self-preservation. The way you throw yourself into danger like you're trying to prove something."

"I'm not Sophia."

"No," he said quietly. "You're something far more dangerous."

"Why?"

He moved so fast I didn't have time to react. One moment he was at the window, the next he had me pressed against his desk, his hands on either side of me, caging me in. I could feel the heat of him, smell that dark scent that clung to him.

"Because Sophia was infatuated with the idea of me," he said, his voice low and rough. "You make me forget why I need to stay away. You make me forget everything except how much I want things I can't have."

My heart was trying to pound its way out of my chest. "Damien..."

"Don't." He pulled back slightly, but didn't move away. His eyes were dark, conflicted, full of want and warning. "We can't."

"Why? Because of some arbitrary rule?"

"Because I'm your professor. Because you're my student. Because the last time I let this happen, someone died."

"I'm not going to die."

"You can't know that."

"And you can't protect everyone by pushing them away."

His control cracked. I saw it in his eyes the moment before he kissed me.

It wasn't gentle. It was fire and desperation and weeks of tension exploding at once. His mouth was demanding, consuming, like he was trying to memorise the taste of me. I fisted my hands in his shirt, pulling him closer, and he groaned against my mouth – a sound that sent heat racing through my veins.

"This is a mistake," he said, but his hands were in my hair, angling my head for better access.

"Probably," I agreed, then bit his lower lip, drawing another one of those sounds from him.

He lifted me onto the desk, stepping between my legs, and I'd never been more grateful for Lilith's dangerously short dress. His mouth moved to my neck, finding that spot where neck meets shoulder that made me gasp, my power flaring involuntarily. The fireplace roared higher, the flames reaching towards the ceiling.

"Control," he murmured against my skin. "You need control."

"I have control."

"No," he said, pulling back to look at me. His lips were swollen from our kiss, his usually perfect hair messed from my fingers. "You don't. Your eyes are literally glowing."

He was right. I could see the orange reflection in his eyes, like tiny flames dancing in the silver.

"Shit."

"Breathe. Pull it back."

I closed my eyes, trying to rein in the fire. It didn't want to listen, fed by adrenaline and desire and the feel of his body against mine. The power wanted out, wanted to burn, wanted to consume everything in its path – including us.

"I can't..."

"Yes, you can." His hands framed my face, gentle now despite the urgency in his voice. "Look at me."

I opened my eyes.

"Breathe with me. In... out... in... out..."

Slowly, painfully, the fire subsided. The glow faded. The room stopped feeling like a furnace. The flames in the fireplace returned to normal size.

"Good girl," he said, and those two words almost undid all my control again. The praise in his voice, the pride in his eyes – it was more intoxicating than the kiss had been.

He stepped back, running both hands through his hair. "This can't happen again."

"Right." My voice came out rougher than intended.

"I mean it, Raven. What we just did... it crossed every line I've sworn not to cross. Every boundary I put in place to protect my students. To protect myself."

"I'm not asking you to be my boyfriend, Damien. I'm not going to write your name in my notebook with little hearts. I'm not Sophia or Amber or any of the others."

"Then what do you want?"

"I want you to stop looking at me like I'm going to break. I want you to teach me everything you know about magic. And I want you to stop pretending you don't feel this too."

"What I feel is irrelevant."

"Bullshit."

"Raven..."

"No. You don't get to kiss me like that and then talk about irrelevance. You want to keep it professional? Fine. But don't insult my intelligence by pretending that was nothing."

He was quiet for a long moment, his jaw working like he was fighting words that wanted to escape. "You're right. It wasn't nothing. Which is exactly why it can't happen again."

"Your call," I said, sliding off the desk and trying to ignore how my legs shook slightly. "But for what it's worth? I think you're so afraid of repeating the past that you're going to miss the present."

I headed for the door, each step feeling like a small victory when all I wanted to do was turn around and throw myself back into his arms.

"Raven."

I paused but didn't turn, my hand on the doorknob.

"Be careful with Victoria. Whatever she's planning, tonight was just the beginning. The truth or dare circle was a test, and you passed. That means she'll escalate."

"I can handle Victoria."

"That's what I'm afraid of."

I left him standing there in the firelight, wondering if I'd just made everything better or infinitely worse. The taste of him lingered on my lips, the feel of his hands in my hair like a ghost of sensation.

The walk back to my dorm was surreal. The party was still going when I passed the west tower, music and laughter spilling out into the night, but it felt like it belonged to a different world – one where professors didn't kiss students, where magic was just fun and games, where lines stayed firmly uncrossed.

But that wasn't my world anymore. Maybe it never had been.

Chapter Eight

Consequences and Conspiracies

The next morning came with a pounding headache and about fifty texts from Iris asking if I was alive, if Darkwood had killed me, or if I'd killed him. There were also several texts that were just strings of question marks and exclamation points.

I stumbled to the communal bathroom, took the world's longest shower trying to wash away the memory of Damien's hands (unsuccessful), and tried not to think about how his mouth had felt against my neck (also unsuccessful).

When I finally made it to the dining hall, the whispers started immediately.

"That's her."

"...in his office for over an hour..."

"...saw them leave together..."

"...Victoria's furious..."

"...heard she cast a beacon spell..."

"...Darkwood actually entered the circle..."

Great. The rumour mill was in full swing, and by lunch, the story would probably involve me seducing him with dark magic while Victoria watched.

I grabbed coffee (black, strong enough to wake the dead) and toast (burnt, because apparently that's my aesthetic now), finding my usual table where Iris, Lilith, and Moon were waiting with eager expressions.

"Spill," Iris demanded before I even sat down. "Everything. Now. Don't leave out a single detail."

"There's nothing to spill."

"You left with Professor Darkwood and didn't come back to the room until 3am," Lilith pointed out, gesturing with a piece of bacon. "I know because I was up doing a ritual and saw you walk of shame-ing down the hallway."

"It wasn't a walk of shame. We talked. About magic. And control."

"Is that what they're calling it now?" Moon asked innocently, though her knowing smile suggested her tarot cards had already told her everything.

Before I could respond, a hush fell over the dining hall like someone had hit a mute button. I looked up to see Headmistress Thornbury standing at the entrance, her steel gaze scanning the room until it landed on me like a searchlight finding an escaped prisoner.

"Ms Blackthorne. My office. Now."

The walk to her office felt like a funeral march. Students stared, some sympathetic, most just grateful it wasn't them. One first year actually crossed herself as I passed, which seemed excessive.

Her office was intimidating as hell – all sharp angles and dark wood, with portraits of previous headmistresses glaring down from the walls. Each portrait's eyes seemed to follow me, and I swear one of them mouthed "troublemaker" as I passed.

"Sit," she commanded.

I sat.

"I've received some disturbing reports about last night."

"It was just a party..."

"With illegal binding circles and compulsion magic." Her voice could have frozen fire. "Both of which are grounds for immediate expulsion. Both of which could result in criminal charges if reported to the Magical Council."

My stomach dropped to somewhere around my feet.

"However," she continued, studying me with those sharp eyes, "I'm told you were a victim, not a perpetrator. Is this accurate?"

"Yes."

"And Professor Darkwood intervened?"

"He broke up the game and made sure everyone was safe."

"How fortunate he happened to be nearby." Her tone suggested she didn't believe in coincidences. She probably didn't believe in accidents either. Or mercy. "Ms Blackthorne, I'm going to be very direct. Are you involved in an inappropriate relationship with Professor Darkwood?"

The question hung in the air like a blade. I could feel the weight of it, the danger. One wrong word and everything would come crashing down.

"No."

"He's providing you with additional training?"

"Yes. To help with control. My magic is... volatile."

"Nothing more?"

I met her gaze steadily, calling on every poker face I'd ever developed in foster care. "Nothing more."

She studied me for a long moment, and I had the uncomfortable feeling she could see straight through me, past the lie, past the truth, right down to my bones.

"Very well. But be advised – I'll be watching. Both of you. One step out of line, and the consequences will be severe. We've lost students before to inappropriate attachments. I won't lose another."

"Lost students?"

"Sophia Colman wasn't the only casualty of dangerous attractions at this academy. Magic and emotion are a volatile combination. When the two become entangled..." She paused, seeming to consider her words. "Let's just say the cemetery isn't merely decorative."

"Is that a threat?"

"It's a warning. And a history lesson." She stood, indicating the meeting was over. "You're dismissed. And Ms Blackthorne? Stay away from binding circles. They have a way of revealing truths better left hidden."

I left her office on shaky legs, only to run into Victoria in the hallway. She was leaning against the wall like she'd been waiting, her perfect nails tapping against the stone in a rhythm that sounded like a countdown.

"Trouble in paradise?" she asked sweetly.

"Shouldn't you be getting expelled? You cast that circle."

"Prove it." She examined her perfect nails like they held the secrets of the universe. "Besides, I'm not the one sneaking around with a professor."

"Neither am I."

"Please. Everyone saw you leave together. Everyone knows what happened."

"Everyone knows what you want them to think happened."

"Same difference." She stepped closer, and I could smell her perfume – something expensive and poisonous. "You may have won our little duel, but this is a different game. Social warfare. Reputation. And in that arena, I'm undefeated."

"Good for you. I don't care about reputation."

"No? Then you won't mind when everyone starts talking about how you're sleeping your way to better grades. How you seduced a professor who has a history of unstable students. How long before people start wondering if you'll end up like Sophia Colman?"

"You're really going there?"

"I'm going wherever it takes to make you leave." Her smile was nothing but edges and malice. "You see, I did some research on you, Raven Blackthorne. Foster kid. Troubled past. Expelled from three high schools for 'incidents'. The car fire wasn't your first, was it?"

My blood went cold. "How do you..."

"My family has resources. Did you know you were flagged by the Magical Council when you were thirteen? 'Potentially dangerous untrained pyrokinetic'. They were considering binding your powers years before Ravenwood intervened."

"That's not..."

"Oh, but it is. You're here on probation, aren't you? One major incident and they'll not just expel you – they'll strip your magic entirely. And what's more major than seducing a professor?"

"I haven't seduced anyone."

"Yet. But you want to. And he wants you to. It's only a matter of time before one of you breaks." She leaned in close. "And when you do, I'll be watching. Waiting. Ready to document every sordid detail."

"You're sick."

"I'm practical. You don't belong here, Blackthorne. You're chaos incarnate. And chaos has no place at Ravenwood."

She walked away, her heels clicking against the stone like a countdown to disaster, leaving me standing in the hallway with a growing sense of dread and the terrible certainty that she was right about one thing – it was only a matter of time before Damien and I broke.

Chapter Nine

The Setup

The next few weeks were hell dressed up in academic robes.

Every time I entered a room, conversations stopped like someone had pulled the plug on a radio. Every time I answered a question in class, someone would mutter about "private tutoring" just loud enough for everyone to hear. Even some professors looked at me differently, like I was a bomb that might go off at any moment.

Professor Ashwood was the worst, taking every opportunity to make cutting remarks.

"Ms Blackthorne," she'd said yesterday, "perhaps you could share with the class the benefits of... personalised instruction? You seem to be quite the expert on the subject."

The class had tittered nervously. I'd set my textbook on fire. Accidentally. Mostly.

Damien had cancelled our private lessons, saying it was "for the best" until things calmed down. He barely looked at me in class, maintaining such a professional distance it was almost insulting. When he did look at me, his expression was carefully neutral, like I was just another student, not someone he'd kissed like the world was ending.

The only people still talking to me normally were my roommates and Iris, who seemed to take the whole situation as a personal challenge.

"We need to fight back," she said, slamming her tray down at lunch hard enough to make her soup splash. "Victoria's controlling the narrative."

"Let her," I said, pushing food around my plate. Even the mashed potatoes looked like they were plotting something.

"You should care," Lilith said, stealing my untouched brownie. "Perception is power here. If everyone thinks you're unstable, they'll treat you like you're unstable. That means partners avoiding you in group work, professors watching you more closely, less access to advanced materials."

"She's systematically isolating you," Moon added, her crystals arranged around her plate in what she claimed was a protective pattern. "It's actually brilliant, in an evil genius way."

"So what do you suggest? I can't exactly prove a negative."

"No," Iris said slowly, a grin spreading across her face that usually meant trouble. "But we can prove Victoria's not as perfect as she pretends to be."

"Iris..."

"Hear me out. Tomorrow night is the new moon. Darkest night of the month. Perfect for sneaking around."

"We're not sneaking anywhere."

"Victoria's been leaving campus every new moon since she got here," Iris continued, ignoring my protest. "Nobody knows where she goes or what she does. But I bet it's not anything the Headmistress would approve of."

"How do you even know this?"

"I have sources. Also, I may have followed her once. Briefly. Until she almost caught me and I had to hide in a tree for three hours."

"You want to follow her?"

"I want to get leverage. She's ruining your reputation. Let's see how she likes having her secrets exposed."

It was petty. It was risky. It was probably stupid.

"Fine."

The next night, we waited in the shadows near the main gate. The new moon made everything darker than usual, and even the stars seemed dimmer. Moon had insisted on casting a concealment charm on us, though I wasn't sure how effective her magic was, given that she'd accidentally turned Iris' hair blue during the spell.

"It's temporary," she'd whispered. "Probably."

Sure enough, at exactly midnight, Victoria slipped out, dressed in all black and moving with purpose. She didn't even look around, confident that no one would dare follow her.

We followed at a distance as she made her way through the woods behind the academy. The path was treacherous in the dark, roots and rocks trying to trip us every few steps. Something howled in the distance, and I tried not to think about the rumours of what lived in these woods.

"Where the hell is she going?" Lilith whispered, pulling her cloak tighter.

"There's nothing out here except..." Iris stopped. "Oh shit."

"What?"

"The old cemetery. The one from before the academy was built. The one where they buried witches who died in the Purge of 1692."

We crept closer, using trees for cover. In a clearing ahead, candles formed a circle around a mausoleum that looked older than the academy itself. The stone was weathered, covered in symbols that seemed to writhe in the candlelight. Victoria stood in the centre, and she wasn't alone.

Five other figures in black robes surrounded her, their faces hidden by hoods. The air was thick with power – old power, the kind that made your teeth ache and your bones feel wrong.

"Is that a coven?" Moon breathed, her concealment charm flickering.

"It's something," I muttered.

Victoria raised her hands, and the others began to chant in a language I didn't recognise. It sounded old, guttural, like words that were never meant to be spoken by human tongues. The air grew thick with power, making my skin prickle. This wasn't light magic. This was something older, darker, something that predated the sanitised magic taught at Ravenwood.

The ground in the centre of their circle began to crack. Something was coming through –

something that should not exist in our world. The temperature dropped twenty degrees in seconds, and frost formed on the grass, sudden and unnatural.

"We need to leave," Lilith said urgently, grabbing my arm. "Now."

But it was too late. One of the hooded figures turned our way, and I felt their awareness hit us like a physical force.

"Someone's here!"

Victoria's head snapped towards us. Even from a distance, I could see her eyes widen in recognition. The concealment charm shattered like glass.

"Run!"

We ran, crashing through the underbrush as shouts erupted behind us. A spell whistled past my ear, singeing the tree beside me and leaving a burn mark that looked disturbingly like a hand print.

"Split up!" I yelled. "Get back to the academy!"

We scattered. I veered left, using my fire to create false trails, walls of flame that would hopefully confuse our pursuers. Behind me, I could hear them crashing through the woods, and something else – something that didn't sound entirely human.

I burst out of the woods near the greenhouse where I'd fought Victoria weeks ago. The irony wasn't lost on me.

"Stop running, Blackthorne."

I spun to find Victoria emerging from the tree line, alone and furious. Her perfect hair was dishevelled, and there was something wild in her eyes.

"You have no idea what you've just done," she said.

"Exposed your little cult? Pretty sure I know exactly what I did."

"It's not a cult, you idiot. It's..." She stopped, tilting her head like she was listening to something. "Someone's coming."

I felt it too – a presence moving through the woods towards us. But it wasn't one of her robed friends. It was something else. Something wrong. The thing they'd been summoning.

"What did you summon?" I asked, my fire already responding to the threat.

"A guardian. A protector. But you interrupted the binding ritual." Her face was pale in the moonlight. "It's not contained. It's not controlled. It's just... hungry."

A shape emerged from the darkness – vaguely humanoid but wrong, like someone had tried to draw a person from memory and messed the proportions up. Its limbs were too long, its head too small, and where its eyes should have been were just holes of pure void. When it opened its mouth, the sound that came out was like breaking glass mixed with screaming wind.

"Can you send it back?"

"Not without the full coven. And not without completing the binding." Victoria raised her hands, light springing to her fingers, but I could see her fear. "We need to hold it until..."

The thing moved faster than thought. One moment it was twenty feet away, the next it had Victoria by the throat, lifting her off the ground like she weighed nothing. Her light flickered and died.

I didn't think. I just acted.

Fire erupted from my hands, not controlled or careful, but raw and wild. The hottest fire I'd ever produced, white-hot with edges of purple and blue. The creature dropped Victoria and turned towards me, apparently deciding I was the bigger threat.

"Bad choice," I muttered, and let my power completely loose.

The fire that came out of me wasn't just fire anymore. It was purification itself, the kind of flame that could burn souls, not just flesh. It hit the creature and kept going, pouring into it, through it, consuming it from the inside out. The thing screamed – a sound that would haunt my nightmares for years – and then imploded, leaving nothing but ash and the smell of sulphur and burnt ozone.

I dropped to my knees, completely drained. Every part of me hurt, like I'd pushed something past its breaking point and maybe broken it permanently. My vision swam, and I could taste copper in my mouth.

"Raven!"

I looked up to see Damien running towards us, followed by the Headmistress and several other professors. Of course they'd felt that much magical discharge. I'd probably lit up every magical sensor within a five-mile radius.

"Are you hurt?" He knelt beside me, his hands checking for injuries with a thoroughness that would have been clinical if not for the tremor in his fingers.

"I'm fine. Just tired. And maybe dying. But mostly tired."

"Ms Ashford," the Headmistress said coldly, ignoring my potential death. "You have significant explaining to do."

Victoria, still rubbing her throat where bruises were already forming, looked between me and the authorities. I could see the calculation in her eyes. She could try to blame this on me, say I was the one performing dark magic. It would be her word against mine, and she had connections, influence, a family name that meant something.

Instead, she straightened and said, "It was my ritual. My responsibility. Raven was just… trying to stop me."

I stared at her in shock.

"We'll discuss this in my office," the Headmistress said. "Both of you. Now."

As Damien helped me to my feet, his arm around my waist the only thing keeping me upright, Victoria caught my eye.

"We're even," she mouthed.

I nodded, too exhausted to argue.

Maybe we were.

Or maybe this was just the beginning of something worse.

Chapter Ten

Truth and Consequences

The Headmistress' office was crowded. Victoria and I sat in chairs facing the desk, though 'sat' was generous in my case – I was more accurately slumped, still feeling like I'd been turned inside out and shaken. Damien stood by the window, his reflection watching us in the dark glass. Two other professors – Grimwood and Ashwood – flanked the door like guards, or witnesses, or both.

"Unauthorised summoning," the Headmistress began, her voice colder than the thing we'd just destroyed, "is not just against academy rules. It's illegal under magical law. The Concordat of 1894 specifically forbids the summoning of entities from the Outer Darkness. Ms Ashford, what you did tonight could result in criminal charges. You could be bound, your magic sealed permanently."

"I understand," Victoria said quietly. She looked smaller than I'd ever seen her, like all her perfect posture had crumbled.

"Do you? Because from where I sit, you've been playing with forces far beyond your comprehension. That creature could have killed someone. Could have killed many someones. Could have broken loose in the academy where hundreds of students sleep."

"It was meant to be a protector..."

"I don't care what it was meant to be. I care about what it became." She turned to me, and I tried to sit up straighter. "Ms Blackthorne, explain your involvement."

I glanced at Victoria, who was staring at her hands like they held the answer to everything. She'd covered for me. The least I could do was return the favour.

"When I saw the creature, I destroyed it."

"How?"

That was the million-dollar question, wasn't it? "I... I'm not sure. I just threw everything I had at it."

Professor Grimwood spoke up, her voice shaking slightly. "That was purifying fire. True purifying fire. It's not something a first year should be able to produce. It requires years of training, decades of practice. Most witches never manage it at all."

"Or exceptional power and desperate circumstances," Damien said, speaking for the first time. "Raven has both."

The Headmistress studied me with those sharp eyes that seemed to see everything. "You realise what you did was incredibly dangerous? Purifying fire can consume the caster if they're not careful. It's not just fire that burns outward – it burns inward too, consuming impurities in the caster's own magic, own soul. Too much, and there's nothing left."

"I didn't exactly have time to be careful."

"No," she agreed. "You didn't." She was quiet for a moment, fingers steepled in front of her face. "Ms Ashford, you're suspended for the remainder of the school year. You'll be allowed to return next year, on probation, with significant restrictions on your magical practice. You will attend mandatory sessions with our counsellor, and you will have a magical monitor placed on you to prevent any unauthorised spellwork."

Victoria nodded, accepting the punishment without argument. "I understand."

"Ms Blackthorne, while your intentions may have been... admirable, your actions were nevertheless against regulations. You will serve detention every weekend for the next month."

"Yes, ma'am."

"Furthermore," she continued, "both of you will sign magical contracts binding you to silence about tonight's events. The last thing this academy needs is panic about dark summonings and ancient entities." She adjusted her robes with sharp, precise movements. "Dismissed. Both of you."

We filed out, Victoria walking quickly ahead. I caught up to her in the hallway, my legs still shaky but functional.

"Victoria, wait."

She stopped but didn't turn.

"Why did you cover for me?"

"You saved my life," she said simply. "Whatever issues we have, that means something. Even in my family, *especially* in my family, life debts are sacred."

"So we're really even?"

She turned then, and for the first time since I'd met her, she looked vulnerable. Really vulnerable, not the calculated vulnerability she sometimes displayed for sympathy. "My grandmother is going to kill me. Literally. The Ashford name, the family reputation... I've ruined it."

"You made a mistake..."

"I've been making mistakes all year." She laughed bitterly. "Do you know why I really hate you?"

"Because I'm better looking?"

Despite everything, she smiled. A real smile, small and sad. "Because you're everything I pretend to be. Powerful without trying. Confident without arrogance. You don't need anyone's approval."

"That's not..."

"It is. And I've spent so much energy trying to tear you down because I was jealous. Because you walked in here on day one and made me feel like a fraud." She straightened, pulling her mask back on piece by piece. "But that ends now. When I come back next year, things will be different."

"Victoria..."

"Take care of yourself, Raven. And... watch out for Scarlett. Without me here to keep her in check, she might cause problems."

"What do you mean?"

"Scarlett's obsessed with Darkwood. Has been since before she came here. She thought I was her ticket to getting his attention – befriend the star student, get close to the professors. When that didn't work..." Victoria shrugged. "Just be careful. Jealousy makes people dangerous."

She walked away before I could respond, her footsteps echoing in the empty hallway.

"That was unexpected."

I turned to find Damien behind me. How did he keep doing that?

"Were you eavesdropping?"

"Ensuring two volatile students didn't start another magical duel in the hallway." He stepped closer, and I could see the concern in his eyes. "Purifying fire, Raven? Do you have any idea how dangerous that was?"

"It worked, didn't it?"

"You could have died. You could have burnt yourself out completely. You could have…"

"But I didn't."

"Through sheer luck…"

"Would you stop?" I snapped, exhaustion making me sharp. "I'm so tired of everyone telling me how lucky I am, how I could have died, how I need to be more careful. I saved Victoria's life. I destroyed that thing. I did what needed to be done."

"You're right," he said quietly. "You did."

The admission surprised me enough that my anger deflated.

"I'm proud of you," he continued. "Terrified by your recklessness, but proud."

"Damien…"

"The Headmistress has reinstated our private lessons. She believes you need additional training to handle your power safely." He paused. "I agree."

"Is that your only reason?"

His eyes darkened. "It's my only reason that matters."

"Liar."

"Saturday, 3pm, my office. Don't be late."

He walked away, leaving me standing in the empty hallway, wondering if things had just got better or more complicated.

Definitely both.

Chapter Eleven

Power Plays

With Victoria gone, the social dynamics at Ravenwood shifted overnight like someone had reshuffled a deck of cards. Her followers scattered like leaves, some trying to cosy up to me (which was hilarious and pathetic in equal measure), others gravitating towards Scarlett, who'd assumed the role of queen bee with disturbing ease.

"She's planning something," Iris warned at breakfast, poking at her eggs suspiciously. "Scarlett's been recruiting."

"Recruiting for what?"

"No idea, but she's been spending a lot of time with the third years. The ones who specialise in mental magic."

Mental magic. Great. Just what I needed – someone poking around in my head, which was already a mess of fire, inappropriate thoughts about my professor, and the lingering echo of that creature's death scream.

"Let her plan," I said, though the words tasted like false bravado. "I've got bigger problems."

Like the fact that my magic had been acting strange since the night with the creature. It came too easily now, too strong. I'd accidentally melted a doorknob yesterday just by touching it while annoyed. This morning, I'd set my alarm clock on fire in my sleep. My dreams were full of flames that burned without heat, consuming everything while leaving it untouched.

"Your power is evolving," Damien explained during our lesson that afternoon. We were in his office, which felt smaller than before, more intimate. Or maybe that was just the weight of what had almost happened here. "Purifying fire changes you. It burns away limitations, but also safeguards."

"Meaning?"

"Meaning you're more powerful but less stable. We need to build new foundations before you lose control completely."

"I'm not going to lose control."

"You melted a doorknob."

"I was annoyed."

"What happens when you're angry? Or scared? Or..." He stopped abruptly.

"Or what?"

"Nothing. Let's focus on meditation exercises."

"You were going to say aroused, weren't you?"

His jaw tightened, that muscle jumping again. "Meditation. Now."

We spent the next hour on breathing exercises that would have been boring as hell if I couldn't feel his eyes on me the entire time. The tension between us had only got worse since that kiss. Every accidental touch sent sparks through me – literal and figurative. The air between us crackled with unspoken words and suppressed desire.

"You're not focusing," he said.

"It's hard to focus when you're staring at me like that."

"Like what?"

"Like you're trying to decide whether to kiss me or lecture me."

"I'm your professor..."

"Unless I request a different advisor for advanced training."

He went very still, like I'd just threatened something precious. "You'd do that?"

"If it meant we could stop pretending this is just about magic, yes."

"Raven..."

The door burst open. Moon stood there, face flushed from running, her usually perfect crystals in disarray.

"We have a problem. It's Lilith."

We found her in our dorm room, sitting on her bed, staring at nothing. Her eyes were blank, pupils dilated to the point where the brown was just a thin ring. She didn't respond to her name, to touch, to Moon waving a hand in front of her face.

"What happened?" I demanded, fear making my fire stir restlessly.

"I don't know," Moon said, tears starting to form. "I came back from class and found her like this. She won't respond to anything. I tried a revival spell, a clarity charm, even threw water on her. Nothing."

Damien knelt in front of Lilith, his expression grim. He passed his hand in front of her face, a faint blue light emanating from his fingers. "Mental magic," he said. "Someone's trapped her in her own mind."

"Scarlett," I growled, fire flickering around my clenched fists.

"You don't know that..."

"Who else would do this? She's been recruiting mental magic users. This is her play."

"Even if it is, we need to focus on helping Lilith first." He stood, and I could see the war in his eyes – between the professor who needed to follow protocol and the man who wanted to hunt down whoever did this. "I need to get Professor Moonwhisper. She specialises in..."

"Wait." Something on Lilith's desk caught my eye. A note, written in elegant script on paper that looked expensive. The kind of paper that came from stores where they asked if you had an appointment just to browse.

Want your friend back? Come to the old greenhouse at midnight. Come alone, or she stays like this forever. – S.

"That bitch," I snarled, fire erupting around my hands before I could stop it. The temperature in the room jumped ten degrees.

"You're not going," Damien said immediately, moving between me and the door like he could physically stop me.

"Like hell I'm not."

"It's obviously a trap..."

"I don't care. She hurt my friend. My roommate. Someone who was kind to me when others weren't. This is my fight."

"Then I'm coming with you."

"The note says alone..."

"I don't care what the note says." His power flared, shadows dancing on the walls. The room actually grew darker, like his magic was eating the light. "You're not facing her alone."

"Damien..."

"This is not a discussion." He turned to Moon, who was clutching her crystals so hard her knuckles were white. "Stay with Lilith. Keep trying revival spells. We'll be back."

"What if you're not?" Moon asked quietly.

"Then get the Headmistress," I said, checking the time. Six hours until midnight. Six hours to prepare for what was obviously a trap. "Tell her everything."

Chapter Twelve

Greenhouse Showdown

The greenhouse looked different at night. More sinister. The broken glass caught moonlight like teeth, and shadows moved in ways shadows shouldn't. The whole structure groaned in the wind, like it was dying slowly, piece by piece.

Scarlett stood in the centre, surrounded by five other students I recognised as third year mental specialists. They formed a loose circle, each one's hands glowing with pale blue light that made their faces look corpselike. The air tasted of ozone and malice.

"You came," Scarlett said, her smile sharp enough to cut. "And you brought him. How predictable."

"Let Lilith go," I said, my fire already stirring, eager for violence.

"After we settle some things." She stepped forward, and I could see the madness in her eyes now, barely contained. "You took everything from me. Damien. Status. Even Victoria preferred you in the end."

"I didn't take anything. You lost them all on your own."

"No. You're a disruption. A chaos agent. Everything was perfect before you arrived."

"Perfect? You were stalking a professor who'd rejected you."

Her face twisted into something ugly. "He didn't reject me. He was waiting. Being professional. Until you showed up with your dangerous magic and your devil-may-care attitude."

"Scarlett," Damien said quietly, and there was something in his voice – pity, maybe. "This needs to stop."

"You're right," she agreed, her smile returning. "It does."

The mental magicians raised their hands in unison. I felt the attack coming – a pressure against my mind, like fingers trying to pry open a door that should stay locked. It was violation in its purest form, someone trying to force their way into the most private part of me.

"Don't fight it," Scarlett said conversationally. "It'll only hurt more if you resist. Just let us in, let us show you what you really are. Let everyone see the truth."

I tried to raise my fire, but the mental assault made it hard to focus. The world tilted sideways. My knees buckled.

"Raven!" Damien moved towards me, but two of the magicians turned their attack on him, and I saw him stagger.

"Did you really think I wouldn't prepare for you?" Scarlett laughed, the sound high and brittle. "I've been planning this for weeks. Studying you both. Your weaknesses. Your patterns. Your feelings for each other."

The pressure increased. I could feel them trying to do to me what they'd done to Lilith – trap me in my own mind, lock me away while my body became an empty shell. They were showing me things, memories twisted into nightmares. The car fire, but this time my sister didn't survive. Foster homes where no one came to save me. Damien turning away in disgust.

But they'd made one mistake.

My mind wasn't a normal mind anymore. The purifying fire hadn't just changed my magic – it had changed me, fundamentally, down to the core of what I was. And when they tried to force their way into my thoughts, they found something they didn't expect.

Fire. Everywhere. Not just regular fire, but the purifying kind. The kind that burnt away everything false, everything imposed, everything that didn't belong.

My mental landscape was an inferno, and they'd just walked right into it.

I heard screaming – not sure if it was them or me or both – and the pressure vanished. When I opened my eyes, three of the mental magicians were on the ground, clutching their heads and moaning. Blood trickled from their noses.

"Impossible," Scarlett uttered, taking a step back.

"You wanted in my head?" I stood, feeling my power surge like a tide. The greenhouse windows that were still intact began to crack from the heat. "Congratulations. How did you like what you found?"

"Take her down!" Scarlett screamed at the remaining magicians, her composure finally cracking completely. "All of you! Now!"

They tried, but they were scared now. Their attack was uncoordinated, weak, like children throwing pebbles at an army tank. I brushed it aside like cobwebs and let my fire loose.

Not at them – I wasn't a killer, no matter what they'd tried to do – but around them. Walls of white-purple flame sprang up, trapping each one in their own personal prison. The heat was intense but not burning, a warning rather than an attack. The message was clear: I could kill you, but I'm choosing not to. This time.

"Let. Lilith. Go." Each word came out accompanied by a pulse of power that made the flames jump higher, reaching towards the greenhouse's destroyed ceiling.

"I can't!" Scarlett backed away, real fear in her eyes now. "The spell – it's locked. Only the caster can release it, and that's…" She pointed at one of the magicians on the ground, a girl who was semiconscious and moaning.

Damien moved to the girl, helping her sit up despite the fact that she'd just tried to attack him. "Release the spell on Lilith. Now."

The girl nodded weakly, her hands glowing briefly before the light faded. "It's done. Please… make the fire stop…"

"Good." I let the fire walls drop, though the temperature remained uncomfortably high. "Now get out. All of you. And if you come near me or my friends again, I won't be so merciful."

They ran, dragging their semiconscious friends with them. Only Scarlett remained, looking between Damien and me with something like heartbreak on her face.

"This isn't over," she said, but the words lacked conviction.

"Yes, it is." Damien's voice was ice to my fire. "You attacked students. Used illegal mental magic. You're done at Ravenwood."

"You'd report me? After everything we…"

"We had nothing, Scarlett. We never did. And what you've become…" He shook his head. "You need help. Professional help. Not revenge."

She laughed, bitter and broken. "You really think you can save her? Your track record isn't great, Damien. How long before she burns out like Sophia? Or worse?"

"That's enough," I said, stepping forward. The ground beneath my feet was starting to char.

"Is it? Has he told you about the others? Not just Sophia and Amber. There was Celestine, who became so dependent on his approval she…"

"Stop." Damien's power flared, shadows writhing like living things. "Leave. Now. Before I forget I'm supposed to be the responsible one."

Scarlett gave us one last look – hurt and fury mixed together – then walked out into the night.

I stood there in the ruined greenhouse, surrounded by scorch marks and broken glass, feeling the adrenaline crash hit like a sledgehammer. My legs shook. My hands trembled. The fire that had felt so controlled moments ago now flickered wildly under my skin.

"You ok?" Damien asked, not moving closer. Smart man.

"Peachy. You?"

"Concerned. What you did – turning mental magic back on the attackers – that shouldn't be possible."

"Add it to the list of impossible things I do before breakfast."

"Raven, I'm serious. Your power is evolving in ways I don't understand. Ways that might be dangerous."

"Everything about me is dangerous. You knew that from day one."

"Yes," he said quietly, finally stepping closer. "I did."

We stood there, inches apart, and I could feel the pull between us – magnetic, inevitable, undeniable.

"We need to check on Lilith," he said.

We walked back to the academy in silence, but it was a different kind of silence. Anticipatory. Electric. Like the moment before lightning strikes.

Chapter Thirteen

Unexpected Allies

Lilith was fine – shaken, pissed off, plotting elaborate revenge, but fine. She'd already started a list titled 'Ways to Destroy Scarlett Without Technically Breaking Any Laws' and was on number thirty-seven when we got back.

"I vote for number twelve," Moon said, reading over her shoulder. "Cursing her to only speak in rhyming couplets is poetic justice."

"Too mild," Lilith said, adding another item to her list. "I was thinking more along the lines of permanent blue hair. Or making everything she eats taste like dirt."

"Ladies," Damien said, though I caught him hiding a smile. "No revenge curses. Ms Morganstern will be dealt with through official channels."

"Boring," Lilith muttered, but she set the list aside.

Scarlett was expelled the next morning. Turns out attacking multiple students with illegal mental magic was the kind of thing even her family's moderate wealth couldn't smooth over. She was gone before lunch, and her followers scattered like roaches when the lights come on, suddenly very interested in keeping their heads down and their magic to themselves.

Which left me in a weird position.

"You're like, the most powerful student here now," Iris said at dinner, gesturing with a french fry. "Everyone knows what you did. How you fought off six mental magicians at once. They're calling you the Mind Burner."

"That's a terrible nickname."

"Better than what they were calling you before," Lilith pointed out. "Professor's Pet had some unfortunate implications."

"The third years are terrified of you," Moon added, absently arranging her peas into a pattern that she claimed would bring good fortune. "I heard some of them talking about transferring."

"Good. Maybe I'll get some peace and quiet."

But peace and quiet wasn't in the cards. Over the next week, I had a steady stream of visitors. Students wanting advice, wanting to learn from me, wanting to be my friend now that I was apparently the biggest badass on campus. It was exhausting.

"Go away," I told the latest group of first years who'd shown up at my door with a plate of cookies and hopeful expressions. "I'm not a mentor, teacher, or role model."

"But you're so powerful..."

"And cranky. Don't forget cranky. Go away."

They went, leaving the cookies. I wasn't too proud to accept baked goods.

"You could be nicer," Moon suggested, already reaching for a cookie.

"I could also set myself on fire and run naked through the halls. Doesn't mean I'm going to."

A knock at the door interrupted my antisocial spiral.

"If that's another first year, I swear..."

I yanked open the door to find Victoria standing there.

She looked different. Her usually perfect appearance was slightly rumpled, like she'd walked here instead of taking a car. Her designer clothes had been replaced with jeans and a jumper that looked comfortable rather than expensive.

"What are you doing here? You're suspended."

"I came to get my things. And to talk to you." She looked past me to my roommates. "Privately, if possible."

My roommates made excuses to leave, though Lilith grabbed the cookie plate on her way out.

"I heard about Scarlett," Victoria said once we were alone.

"News travels fast."

"She always was unstable. I tried to keep her in check, but..." She shrugged. "Without me here, she spiralled."

"Not your fault."

"Isn't it? I created the environment that let her thrive. The hierarchy, the power plays, the competition. I set the stage for this."

"You didn't make her attack Lilith."

"No, but I made it seem acceptable to use power against those we saw as lesser." She sat on my bed, and it was strange seeing her in my space, human and vulnerable instead of perfect and untouchable. "I've had a lot of time to think. About what I want, who I want to be."

"And?"

"I want to apologise. Properly. For everything. The harassment, the rumours, the Circle that first night."

"Victoria..."

"I was threatened by you from the moment you arrived. You had raw power I'd worked years to achieve. You stood up to me when everyone else cowered. You made me feel small, and I hated you for it."

"I wasn't trying to..."

"I know. That almost made it worse. You weren't even trying, and you still outshone me." She laughed, but it wasn't bitter. "My grandmother was furious about the suspension. Threatened to disown me. Cut me off. Make me get a regular job like a regular person."

"Harsh."

"Then I told her about the creature, how you saved my life with purifying fire. Do you know what she said?"

"What?"

"'Perhaps you could learn something from this Blackthorne girl.' The great Evangeline Ashford, suggesting I learn from you. From someone she would have called scum of the earth a month ago."

"That must have stung."

"It did. But she was right. I've spent so much time maintaining my image that I forgot to develop my actual self. I've been so focused on being perfect that I forgot to be real." She stood. "When I come back next year, I want to start over. Really start over. Think you could handle being friends with a reformed mean girl?"

"Friends might be pushing it. But not enemies? That I could do."

She smiled – a real smile, not her practiced one. "I'll take it." She headed for the door, then paused. "Oh, and Raven? Whatever's going on with you and Professor Darkwood?"

"Nothing's going on..."

"Please. The sexual tension could power the entire academy. The air literally shimmers when you two are in the same room." She turned to face me fully. "Just... be careful. He's a good man, but he carries a lot of guilt. Don't let him push you away because he thinks he's protecting you."

"Speaking from observation?"

"Speaking from experience. I had a crush on him a long time ago. He let me down gently, but I saw how he looked at Sophia. And now how he looks at you. It's different. Deeper. Like you're not just another powerful student to him."

"What do you mean?"

"I mean he looks at you like you're the answer to a question he didn't know he was asking. Don't let him sabotage it."

She left before I could respond, leaving me standing there wondering if Victoria Ashford had just given me relationship advice.

The world had officially gone insane.

Chapter Fourteen

Breaking Points

Some days were torture, each private lesson an exercise in self-control. The tension between Damien and me had reached ridiculous levels. We couldn't even be in the same room without the air crackling with suppressed energy.

"Focus," he said for the tenth time that afternoon.

"I am focused."

"Your fire says otherwise."

He was right. The flames I was supposed to be shaping into a weapon kept forming other things. Abstract shapes that looked suspiciously like two figures entwined. Today they were particularly obvious, and I could feel my face burning with embarrassment.

"Sorry." I dissipated the flames, trying to think of anything except the way his shirt stretched across his shoulders when he moved.

"You're distracted."

"By what?" I asked innocently.

"Seriously?" He sighed, running a hand through his hair in that way that meant he was frustrated. With me, with himself, with the situation – probably all three. "We should stop for today. You're not going to improve with your concentration this scattered."

"My concentration is fine. You're the one who keeps forgetting what you're saying mid-sentence when I stretch."

"I don't..." He stopped, and I watched realisation dawn on his face. "You're doing that on purpose?"

"The stretching? Maybe." I demonstrated, arching my back in a way that was definitely not necessary for any magical exercise.

"You're impossible."

"And you're attracted to impossible."

"Raven…"

The door burst open. A second year student I vaguely recognised stood there, panicked and out of breath.

"Professor, we need help. There's something wrong with the protection circles. They're failing."

We ran.

The protection circles were Ravenwood's first line of defence – ancient magic woven into the very foundations of the academy. They kept out malevolent spirits, hostile magic, and uninvited guests. They were supposed to be unbreakable, maintained by centuries of accumulated power.

They were also completely down.

"How?" Headmistress Thornbury demanded, standing at the main gate where the circles should have been visible as a faint shimmer in the air. Now there was nothing, just empty space where our defences should be.

"I don't know," Professor Grimwood said, wringing her hands. "They were fine this morning. I checked them myself as part of my routine."

"Someone sabotaged them," Damien said, kneeling to examine the anchor stones embedded in the ground. They were cracked, black veins spreading through the crystal. "From the inside. This was deliberate. This took time, planning, and considerable power."

"Who would..."

A laugh cut through the air. High, unhinged, familiar.

Scarlett stood at the tree line, but she wasn't alone. Behind her were figures in black robes. The same robes from Victoria's ritual. The same ones from the old cemetery.

My blood went cold.

"Did you think expelling me would make me go away?" she called out, her voice carrying on the wind. "Did you think I'd just accept it? Crawl away in shame?"

"Ms Morganstern," the Headmistress said coldly, though I could see tension in her shoulders. "You're trespassing."

"Am I? With no protection circles, this is just property. And I have friends who've been dying to visit."

The robed figures moved forward, and I realised they weren't students. They were older, more powerful, and their magic felt wrong. Dark. Hungry. Ancient in a way that made my teeth ache.

"Practicing witches who've been rejected by the academic establishment," Scarlett explained, her smile manic. "They have grievances. Years of being told their magic was wrong, dark, forbidden. I offered them a chance for revenge."

"You've lost your mind," Damien said, moving protectively closer to me.

"Have I? Or have I finally found people who appreciate my talents?" She raised her hands, and darkness – true darkness, not just absence of light – poured from her fingers. "They taught me things. Things the academy would never teach. Want to see?"

The darkness moved like liquid, reaching for us with tendrils that whispered of madness and despair. It wasn't just dark – it was the concept of darkness, the idea of void given form.

I threw fire at it, but the darkness swallowed it whole, consuming it without even a flicker.

"Your fire can't burn what isn't there," Scarlett laughed. "And soon, none of you will be either."

The robed figures attacked. Not with fire or lightning or any magic I recognised, but with entropy itself. Things aged, crumbled, decayed wherever their spells touched. A section of the academy wall aged a hundred years in seconds, crumbling to dust.

"Fall back!" the Headmistress ordered. "Defensive positions!"

But there was nowhere to fall back to. With the protection circles down, they could follow us anywhere on academy grounds. We were exposed, vulnerable, defenceless.

"We need to restore the circles," Damien said urgently.

"That would take hours…"

"Not if we had enough power." He looked at me, and I saw the idea form in his eyes. "Raven, the purifying fire. It could cleanse the anchor stones, reset them."

"I don't know how…"

"I do. But I need your power. All of it."

"That's insane," Professor Grimwood protested, backing away from an entropy spell that turned the grass beneath it to ash. "The amount of power required…"

"Would kill a normal witch," Damien agreed. "But Raven's not normal."

Another wave of darkness crashed towards us. Other professors threw up shields, but they were already weakening, cracking under the assault.

"Do it," I said.

Damien grabbed my hands, and the connection was immediate, electric. "This is going to hurt."

"Everything good does."

He smiled grimly, then opened his power to mine.

It was like touching a live wire and diving into an ocean at the same time. His magic – controlled, disciplined, structured – met my chaos fire, and instead of fighting, they merged. They fitted together like pieces of a puzzle I hadn't known existed.

I could feel him in my mind, not invasive like the mental magicians, but supportive. Guiding. Together, we reached for the broken anchor stones scattered around the academy's perimeter.

The purifying fire erupted from us – from me, through him, shaped by our combined will. It raced along the academy's foundations, finding each anchor stone, burning away the corruption Scarlett had introduced. But it was more than that. The fire was cleaning years of accumulated darkness, centuries of small corruptions that had built up over time.

Damien was right – it hurt. Like being turned inside out while on fire. Like every cell in my body was being reconstructed from scratch. I could feel myself fragmenting, dissolving into pure energy.

"Hold on," he said, his voice in my head more than my ears. His presence was the only thing keeping me anchored, keeping me from disappearing entirely into the flame. "Almost there."

The last anchor stone ignited, and the protection circles snapped back into place with a sound like thunder. But they were different now – stronger, purified, glowing with white-purple fire.

The robed figures' spells hit the restored barriers and bounced back, their own entropy consuming them. They fled, screaming, leaving Scarlett alone at the tree line.

"This isn't over!" she shrieked. "I'll find another way! I'll…"

The Headmistress flicked her wrist, and Scarlett froze mid-sentence, encased in a crystal prison.

"Aurors from the Magical Council will be here shortly," she said calmly, as if she hadn't just been fighting for the academy's survival. "Attacking an academy is a high crime, Ms Morganstern. You'll have years in prison to reconsider your choices."

I would have been more interested in Scarlett's fate if I wasn't busy trying not to die. The world spun, my knees buckled, and only Damien's arms kept me upright. I could feel something inside me breaking, some fundamental limit I'd pushed too far.

"I've got you," he murmured, scooping me up like I weighed nothing.

"Did we win?"

"We won."

"Good. I'm going to pass out now."

"I've got you," he repeated, and it was the last thing I heard before darkness claimed me.

Chapter Fifteen

Revelations

I woke up in the infirmary with the worst magical hangover of my life. Everything hurt, even my hair. My mouth tasted like I'd been eating ash, and my magic felt... different. Quieter, maybe. Or just exhausted.

"She's awake!"

I groaned as Iris' voice pierced my skull like a nail. "Volume," I croaked.

"Sorry," she whispered, though her version of whispering was still too loud. "You've been out for three days. We were getting worried."

"Three days?"

"You channelled enough power to restart the entire protection circle system," Lilith said, appearing at my other side. "That's like, deity-level magic. They're already adding it to the academy history books."

"It felt like dying-level magic."

"The Headmistress wants to see you when you're up for it," Moon added, fussing with the crystals she'd arranged around my bed in what looked like a healing pattern. "And Professor Darkwood hasn't left the infirmary. He's been sleeping in that chair."

I turned my head – ow – and saw him. He was slumped in a visitor's chair, still in the same clothes from three nights ago, stubble darkening his jaw. He looked exhausted, vulnerable in a way I'd never seen him.

"He looks like hell," I observed.

"He wouldn't leave," the nurse said, bustling over to check my vitals with various magical instruments that hummed and glowed. "Kept saying he needed to make sure you were stable. As if I don't know how to do my job. I've been healing magical injuries since before he was born."

"Can you give us a minute?"

She huffed but herded my friends out, muttering about young people and their drama.

"Damien," I called softly.

His eyes snapped open, immediately finding mine. The relief in them was almost painful to see. "You're awake."

"Disappointed?"

"Relieved." He moved to sit on the edge of my bed, his hand finding mine. "You scared me."

"Big bad professor was scared?"

"Terrified." His thumb traced circles on my palm. "When you collapsed, when you wouldn't wake up... I thought I'd pushed you too far. Asked too much. I thought I'd killed you."

"You didn't ask. I volunteered."

"Still."

"Damien, we saved the academy."

"*You* saved the academy. I just directed the power."

"Our power. It worked because we did it together. Because we're..." I struggled for the right word. "Compatible."

He was quiet for a moment, his eyes studying our joined hands. "The Headmistress knows. About us. About... feelings being involved."

My stomach dropped. "And?"

"She's agreed to transfer you to Professor Moonwhisper for advanced training."

"What? No. I don't want..."

"It's for the best."

I sat up, ignoring the way the room spun and my vision went grey at the edges. "Don't you dare."

"Raven..."

"No. Don't you dare push me away now. Not after everything. Not after we literally combined our magic to save everyone."

"I'm not pushing. I'm being practical."

"Bullshit. You're being scared."

His jaw tightened. "Of course I'm scared. You almost died channelling power through our connection. What happens next time? What happens when..."

I kissed him. It was probably a terrible idea, given that I'd been unconscious for three days and probably had the worst morning breath in history, but I didn't care. I needed him to stop talking, stop thinking, stop being afraid.

He resisted for about half a second, then his hand was in my hair and he was kissing me back like a drowning man who'd found air. Like he'd thought he'd never get to do this again.

The door opened, and we sprang apart like guilty teenagers.

The Headmistress stood there, one eyebrow raised. "I see you're feeling better, Ms Blackthorne."

"Much," I said, trying not to blush and failing spectacularly.

"Good. We have matters to discuss." She looked at Damien. "Alone, Professor Darkwood."

He squeezed my hand once, then left, though I could feel his reluctance.

"So," the Headmistress said once he was gone. "You and Professor Darkwood."

"There's nothing..."

"Please. I'm old, not blind. I've been watching this develop since your first day." She moved closer, her expression softer than I'd ever seen it. "However, given that you saved the academy, and that Professor Darkwood has endeavoured to maintain professional boundaries despite obvious personal feelings, I'm willing to be... flexible."

"Flexible how?"

"Complete your first year. Maintain your grades. Refrain from engaging in any relationship while you remain his student. Fulfil these conditions, and I will not stand in your way come summer."

"That's... surprisingly reasonable."

"I was young once, Ms Blackthorne. I understand the power of connection, especially magical connection. What you and Professor Darkwood achieved together was remarkable. It would be foolish to discourage such compatibility."

"Thank you."

"Don't thank me yet. Your power has grown exponentially. You'll need additional training, more than we can provide here."

"What do you mean?"

"There's a summer programme. Advanced study with the Magical Council. It's intensive, challenging, and will separate you from everyone here for two months."

"Including Damien?"

"Including Professor Darkwood, yes. But when you return, you'll be better equipped to handle your abilities. And," she smiled slightly, "no longer his student in any capacity."

"When would I leave?"

"The day after the end of this academic year."

So much for summer with Damien. But maybe that was for the best. Time to get my power under control, to figure out who I was without the constant distraction of him.

"I'll do it."

"Excellent. Now, get dressed. You have classes to catch up on. Your friends have been taking notes, but I'm afraid you've missed several important lessons."

Chapter Sixteen

Final Weeks

The last three weeks of the academic year flew by in a blur of finals, practical exams, and carefully maintained distance from Damien. We were professional to a fault in public, which somehow made everything worse. Every accidental touch in passing burned. Every formal "Ms Blackthorne" and "Professor Darkwood" felt like foreplay.

"The sexual tension is literally making the air shimmer," Iris complained after watching us have a perfectly professional conversation about my final project. "Just bang already."

"Two more days," I muttered, for what felt like the thousandth time.

"You're a better woman than me. I would have jumped him in the supply closet by now."

"The thought has crossed my mind. Several times. Per day."

The night before the last day of classes, I couldn't sleep. I stood on the roof of my dorm, practicing fire forms, trying to burn off nervous energy. The flames came easier now, more controlled but also more powerful. The purifying fire had changed them, changed me.

"You should be resting."

I didn't turn. "So should you."

Damien stepped beside me, maintaining careful distance. Always maintaining distance. "Tomorrow."

"Tomorrow you're still my professor."

"Tomorrow night I'm not."

"11:59pm, you'll still be..."

"My quarters. Midnight. Not a second before."

I turned to look at him. "Seriously?"

"I've waited this long to do this right. I can wait another twenty-four hours."

"You're assuming I'll show up."

"You will." The confidence in his voice should have been annoying. Instead, it sent heat racing through me.

"Cocky."

"Confident." He stepped back, and I could see the effort it took. "One more day, Raven. Then no more rules, no more boundaries, no more pretending."

He left me on the roof, counting stars and hours, my fire dancing around me in patterns that looked suspiciously like hearts. I'd deny it if anyone asked.

The last day of classes was torture. I sat through my final exam in Damien's class, hyperaware of every movement he made. He was careful not to look at me too often, but when he did, the heat in his eyes made me forget my own name. I'm pretty sure I spelt it wrong on my exam.

"Time," he called, his voice perfectly professional.

Everyone handed in their papers. I was last, placing mine on his desk, our fingers brushing for just a moment. The contact sent electricity up my arm.

"Ms Blackthorne," he said formally, though his eyes were anything but formal. "Have a good summer."

"You too, Professor."

I left without looking back, though every step felt like walking through quicksand.

The rest of the day dragged. Dinner felt endless. My roommates' goodbye party – sweet as it was – seemed to last forever. They'd decorated our room with magical streamers that wrote embarrassing messages in the air, and Moon had made a cake that literally sparkled.

"I'm going to miss you," she said, hugging me tightly. "Promise you'll write from the Council programme."

"I'll try, but I don't know if they allow outside communication."

"You'll be brilliant," Lilith said, joining the hug. "Show those Council stiffs what real power looks like."

"Don't burn down any buildings," Iris added, making it a group hug. "Or at least, don't get caught."

Finally, *finally*, it was 11:45.

I stood outside his quarters, watching the clock like it held the secrets of the universe. 11:57. 11:58. 11:59…

The door opened before I could knock.

"Midnight," Damien said, pulling me inside. "You're officially not my student."

"Thank God."

We crashed together like waves against rocks, like stars colliding, like every cliché I'd ever rolled my eyes at suddenly making perfect sense. Months of tension, want, and careful control shattered in an instant. His hands were everywhere – my hair, my waist, pulling me impossibly closer. Mine were busy too, finally getting to touch what I'd been staring at for months.

"I've wanted this since the first day," he said against my neck, finding that spot that made me gasp. "You walked into orientation with that attitude, that power, and I knew I was in trouble."

"Good trouble?"

"The best trouble." His mouth found mine again, and coherent thought became impossible.

Clothes disappeared with embarrassing speed. We didn't make it to the bedroom, barely made it to the couch. Everything was heat and need. His hands on my skin felt like coming home and setting the house on fire at the same time. Every touch was electric, every kiss a promise, every gasp a confession.

When he touched me, really touched me, my magic responded, filling the room with warmth and light. When I touched him back, shadows danced with flames on the walls, our magic intertwining as thoroughly as our bodies.

"You're going to be the death of me," he gasped against my shoulder.

"But what a way to go," I managed, before speech became impossible again.

Later, much later, we lay tangled together on his bed (we'd eventually made it there), my head on his chest, his fingers tracing lazy patterns on my bare shoulder. I could hear his heartbeat, still faster than normal, and felt ridiculously proud of that.

"So," I said, tracing the defined muscles of his chest, marvelling that I was finally allowed to do this. "Worth the wait?"

"Worth everything." He pressed a kiss to my hair. "Worth every moment of torture, every cold shower, every night I lay awake thinking about this."

"Even the almost dying?"

"Let's not make that a habit."

"Deal." I traced a scar on his ribs I hadn't noticed before. "What's this from?"

"Training accident when I was younger."

"Seriously?"

"I was young and stupid and trying to impress a girl."

"Did it work?"

"No. She thought I was an idiot. She was right."

"I think scars are sexy."

"Of course you do." He rolled us so he was above me, his weight a delicious pressure. "You think danger is sexy."

"I think you're sexy."

"That too," he agreed, then proceeded to show me exactly how sexy he found me in return.

After wanting each other for so long, we didn't sleep that night. Two months of separation lay ahead. We made every hour count, learning each other's bodies like spells to master, territories to claim.

When dawn came, painting the room in soft gold, I was wrapped around him like a vine, unable to tell where I ended and he began.

"I leave tonight," I said quietly.

"I know."

"Two months."

"You'll be brilliant. The Council's programme is exactly what you need. You'll learn control, advanced techniques, things I could never teach you."

"Will you miss me?"

He tilted my chin up, his eyes serious. "Every second. Every heartbeat. I'll count the days until you come back to me."

"Good. Because if I come back and find out you've replaced me with another dangerous first year…"

He kissed me quiet, thoroughly, until I forgot what I was saying. "Never. You've ruined me for normal witches. For anyone who isn't you."

"I was never normal."

"No," he agreed, running his hands through my thoroughly messed hair. "You're extraordinary. My extraordinary disaster."

We talked about everything and nothing. He told me about his childhood, learning magic from his grandmother who was even stricter than Thornbury. I told him about foster homes and discovering my power the hard way. We made love again, slower this time, memorising each other for the separation ahead.

In the calm that followed, he held me like he was afraid I'd disappear.

"Promise me something," he said.

"What?"

"Be careful at the Council. Don't take unnecessary risks. Come back to me whole."

"I promise. If you promise something too."

"Anything."

"Don't close yourself off while I'm gone. Don't convince yourself this was a mistake. Don't let guilt or fear make you push me away when I come back."

He was quiet for a long moment. "I promise."

"Good. Because I love you, and I'd hate to have to burn down your office to prove it."

He went very still. "What?"

"I love you. Deal with it."

"Say it again."

"I love you, Damien Darkwood. I love your stupid need for control and your dramatic entrances and the way you look at me like I'm dangerous and precious at the same time."

"Raven..." His voice was rough with emotion.

"You don't have to say it back. I just needed you to know..."

"I love you too. God help me, I love you. I've been fighting it for months, but it's like fighting gravity. Impossible and pointless."

"Such romantic words."

"Would you prefer poetry?"

"I'd prefer you show me again how much you love me."

He did. Thoroughly.

Epilogue

Coming Home

Two months later, I stood at the gates of Ravenwood again. Same gothic architecture, same sense of foreboding, but I was different. Stronger. More controlled. The Council's programme had been brutal but effective. I could now create fire in seven different colours, each with different properties. I could burn specific things while leaving others untouched. I could even, on good days, create solid constructs from flame.

But more importantly, I understood my power now. Understood its roots, its dangers, its potential.

"Raven!"

Iris tackled me in a hug, followed quickly by Lilith and Moon, who'd all arrived early to greet me.

"You look different," Moon said, studying me with those mystic eyes. "More... centred? Balanced? Like your chakras finally aligned."

"Two months of meditation and advanced training will do that."

"Boring," Lilith declared. "Please tell me you're still the chaotic badass we know and love."

"Would I be anything else?" I demonstrated by creating a small phoenix from purple fire that landed on her shoulder.

"Ok, that's actually cool."

"Ladies."

We all turned. Damien stood there, and my heart did something stupid in my chest that the Council's training definitely hadn't fixed. Two months of video calls hadn't prepared me for seeing him in person again. He was wearing all black, as usual, but his eyes were warm as they found mine.

"Professor," my friends chorused, then made obvious excuses to leave.

"That's our cue," Iris said, dragging the others away. "We'll catch up later, Raven. Much later. Like tomorrow. Or next week."

We stood there, feet apart, drinking each other in. He looked good. Really good. The summer sun had given him a slight tan that made his eyes stand out even more.

"Hi," I said brilliantly.

"Hi."

"So..."

He closed the distance in two strides, kissing me in full view of anyone who cared to look. It was a claiming kiss, a welcome-home kiss, a statement to anyone watching that I was his and he was mine.

When we finally broke apart, half the returning students were staring, mouths open.

"That's going to cause gossip," I said, though I couldn't stop smiling.

"Let them talk." He threaded his fingers through mine. "I'm done hiding this. Done pretending you're not the most important thing in my world."

"The Headmistress…"

"Has already approved. You're not my student anymore. You're an advanced practitioner here for specialised training. Different rules."

Victoria chose that moment to walk by, back from her suspension. She looked between us, shook her head with a smile, and called out, "About damn time! The sexual tension was making it hard to focus in class!"

Several other students voiced their agreement.

"Wow," I said. "Even the former mean girl approves."

"I don't care who approves." He kissed me again, softer this time. "Welcome home, Raven."

Home. It was strange to think of Ravenwood that way, but he was right. Somewhere between that first day and now, between fire and friendship and nearly dying to save this place, it had become home.

But more than that, *he* had become home. My anchor in the chaos, my control in the fire, my match in every way that mattered.

"Come on," I said, tugging him towards the building. "I want to see what chaos I can cause in my second year."

"Of course you do."

"You love it."

"I love you."

"Same thing."

We walked into Ravenwood together, hand in hand, ready for whatever came next. The other students parted for us, some whispering, some smiling, some looking scandalised.

After all, I was Raven Blackthorne. I'd faced down mean girls, dark creatures, and rogue witches. I'd nearly died saving the academy. I'd mastered purifying fire and caught the heart of the most dangerous professor on campus.

Year two was going to be interesting.

But then again, with me and Damien together?

It was going to be absolutely incendiary.

And I wouldn't have it any other way.

THE END

Author's Note: Thank you for reading Pure Magic! This has been Raven Blackthorne's complete story – a standalone tale of magic, fire, and love that burns brighter than any flame. From her first defiant day at Ravenwood Academy to finding both her power and her match in Damien Darkwood, Raven has proven that sometimes the most dangerous magic is the kind that brings two souls together.

While Raven and Damien's story is complete, Ravenwood Academy holds many more secrets. But for now, our firecracker witch and her brooding professor have earned their happily ever after – even if it's likely to include a few more explosions along the way.

After all, what's true love without a little danger?